THE SECRET OF THE STONE FROG

A TOON GRAPHIC NOVEL BY

DAVID NYTRA

TOON BOOKS • NEW YORK

ALSC GRAPHIC NOVELS READING LIST (2016)

CONNECTICUT STATE NUTMEG BOOK AWARD NOMINEE (2015)

HARVEY AWARD NOMINEE (2013)

BOOKLIST TOP 10 BOOKS FOR YOUTH, GRAPHIC NOVELS (2013)

THE NEW YORK PUBLIC LIBRARY'S CHILDREN'S BOOK
LIST OF 100 TITLES FOR READING AND SHARING (2012)

SCHOOL LIBRARY JOURNAL'S TOP TEN GRAPHIC NOVELS (2012)

A JUNIOR LIBRARY GUILD SELECTION

For Mama and Papa

Also look for: WINDMILL DRAGONS,
a Leah and Alan Adventure, by the same author.

Editorial Director: FRANÇOISE MOULY

Guest Editors: NADJA SPIEGELMAN & JULIA PHILLIPS

Book Design: TRACY SUNRIZE JOHNSON

DAVID NYTRA'S artwork was drawn with a crowquill pen and india ink on board.

A TOON Book™ © 2012 David Nytra & RAW Junior, LLC, 27 Greene Street, New York, NY 10013. No part of this book may be used or reproduced in any manner whatsoever without written permission except in the case of brief quotations embodied in critical articles and reviews. TOON Graphics™, TOON Books®, LITTLE LIT® and TOON Into Reading!™ are trademarks of RAW Junior, LLC. All rights reserved. Library of Congress Cataloging-in-Publication Data: Nytra, David, 1977– The Secret of the Stone Frog : a TOON book / by David Nytra.   p. cm.
Summary: Siblings Leah and Alan wake one morning in the middle of an enchanted forest and encounter a strange and spectacular world filled with foppish lions, giant rabbits, and a talking stone frog for a guide. ISBN 978-1-935179-18-4 1. Graphic novels. [1. Graphic novels. 2. Fantasy. 3. Brothers and sisters--Fiction.] I. Title. PZ7.7.N98Se 2012   741.5'973--dc23   2011050431
All our books are Smyth Sewn (the highest library-quality binding available) and printed with soy-based inks on acid-free, woodfree paper harvested from responsible sources. Printed in China by C&C Offset Printing Co., Ltd. Distributed to the trade by Consortium Book Sales & Distribution, a division of Ingram Content Group; orders (866) 400-5351; ips@ingramcontent.com; www.cbsd.com.

ISBN: 978-1-935179-18-4 (hardcover)   ISBN: 978-1-943145-46-1 (softcover)

19 20 21 22 23 24 C&C 10 9 8 7 6 5 4 3

WWW.TOON-BOOKS.COM

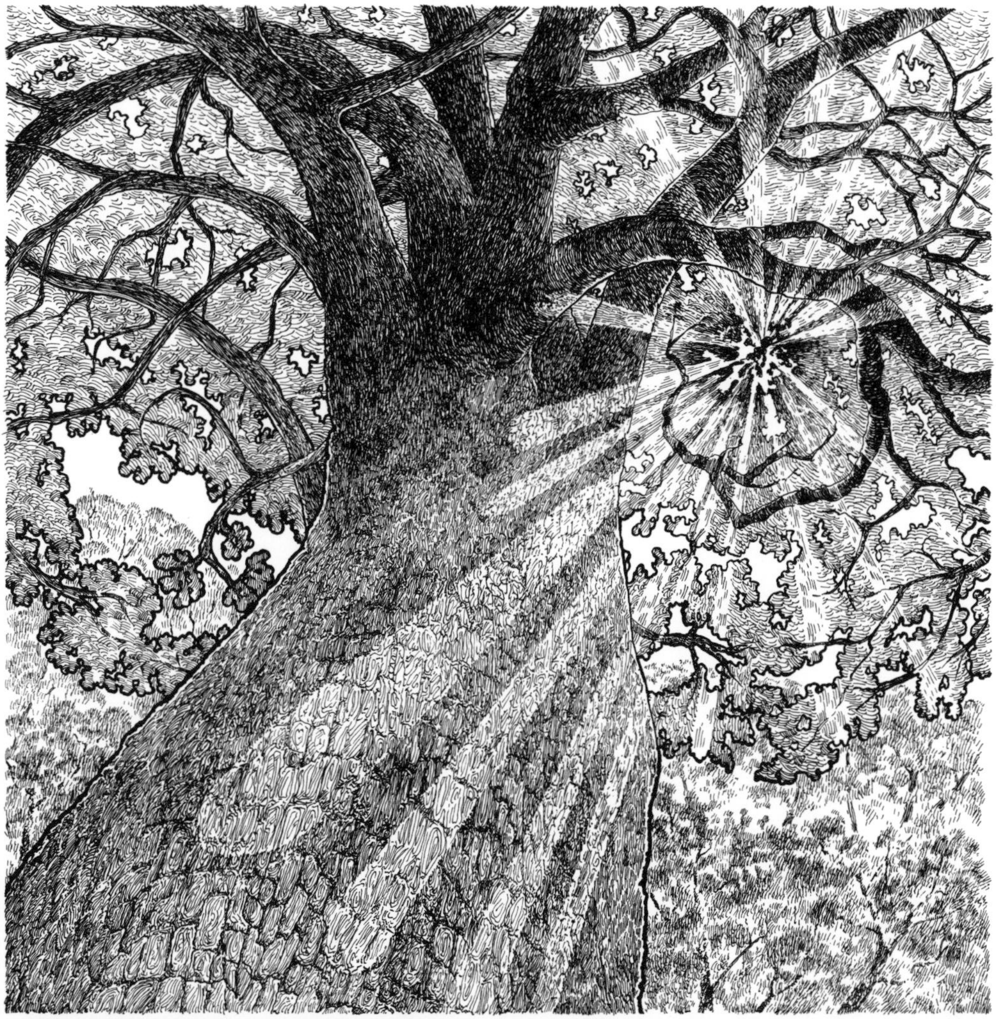

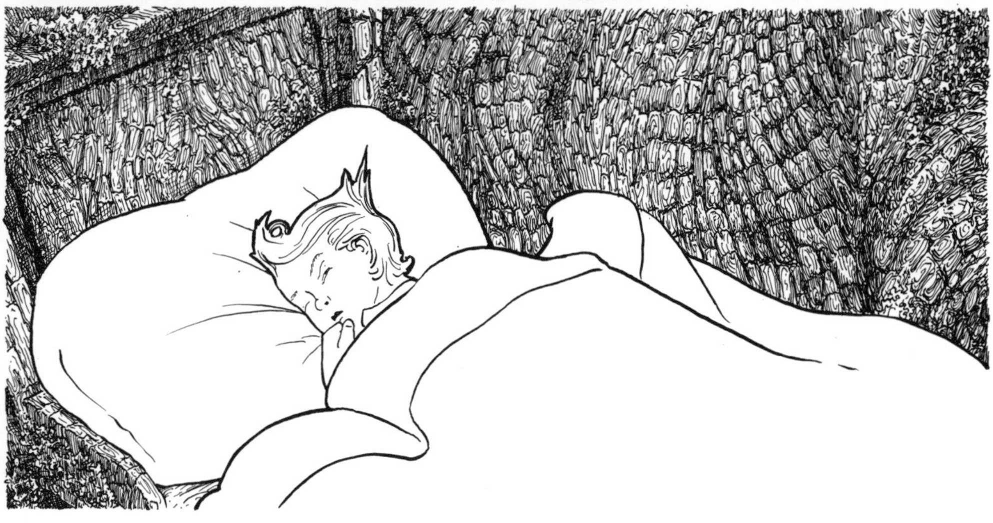

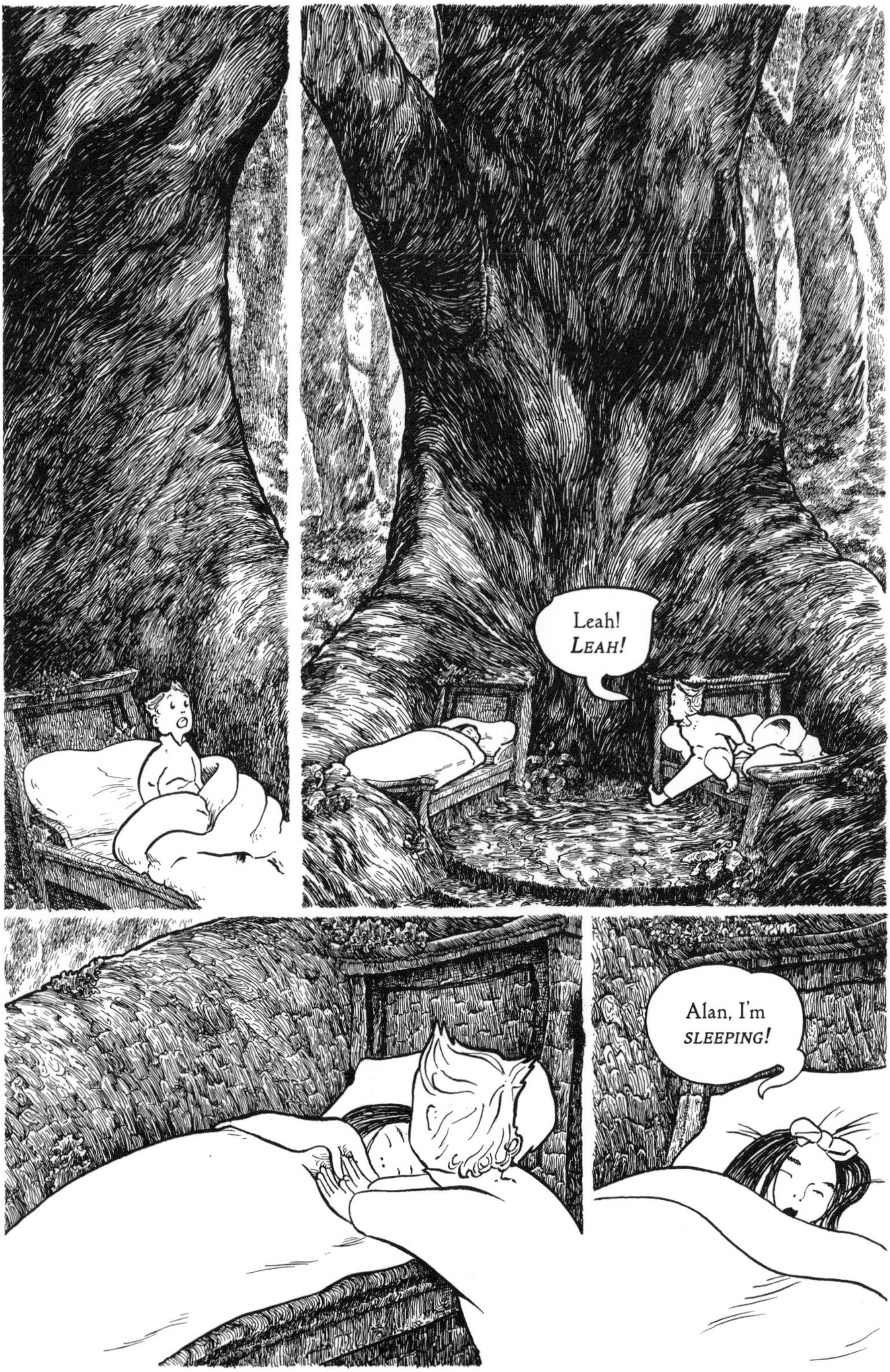
Leah!
LEAH!
Alan, I'm
SLEEPING!

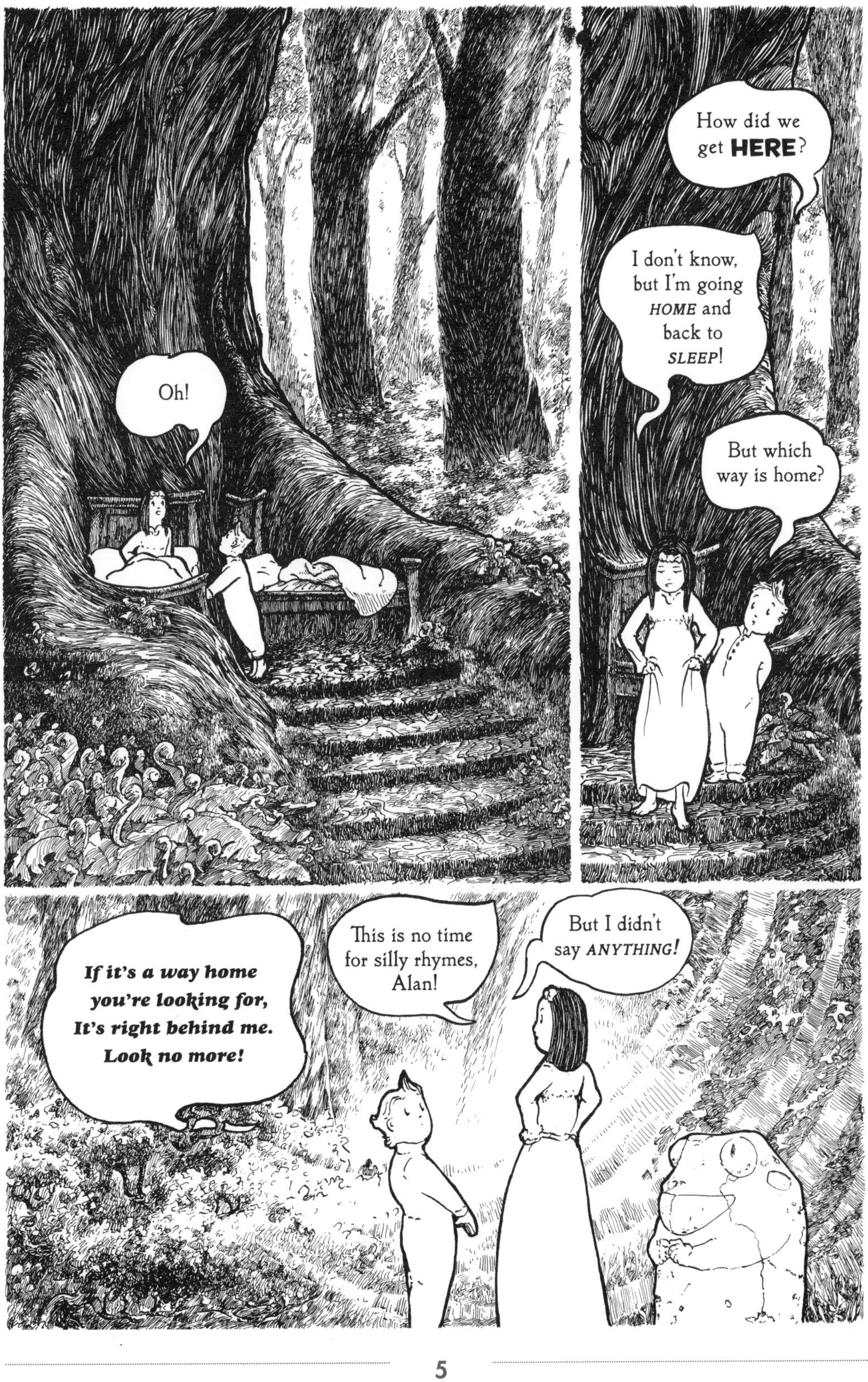
Oh!
How did we get HERE?
I don't know, but I'm going HOME and back to SLEEP!
But which way is home?
If it's a way home you're looking for, It's right behind me. Look no more!
This is no time for silly rhymes, Alan!
But I didn't say ANYTHING!

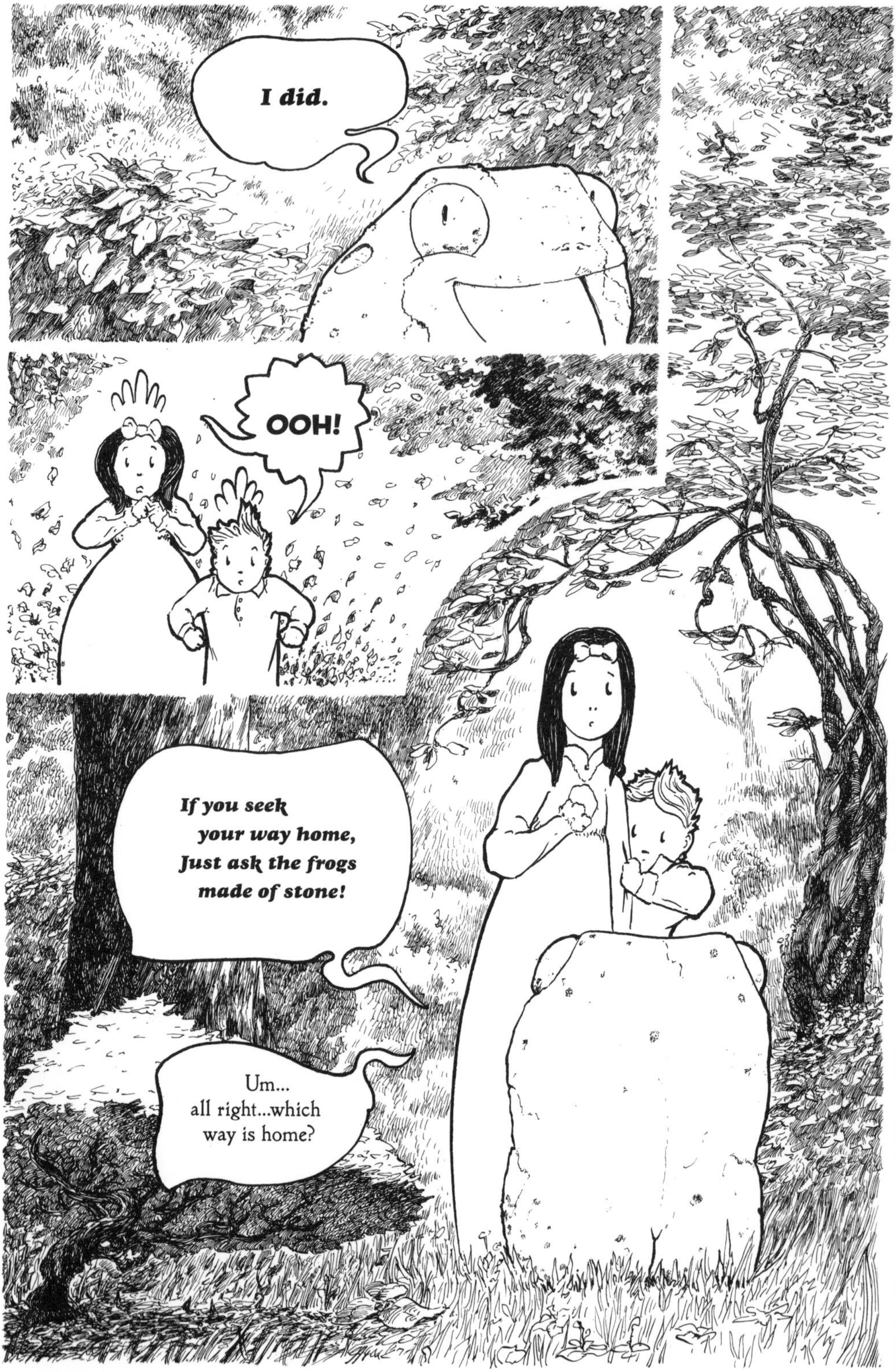
I did.
OOH!
If you seek your way home, Just ask the frogs made of stone!
Um... all right...which way is home?

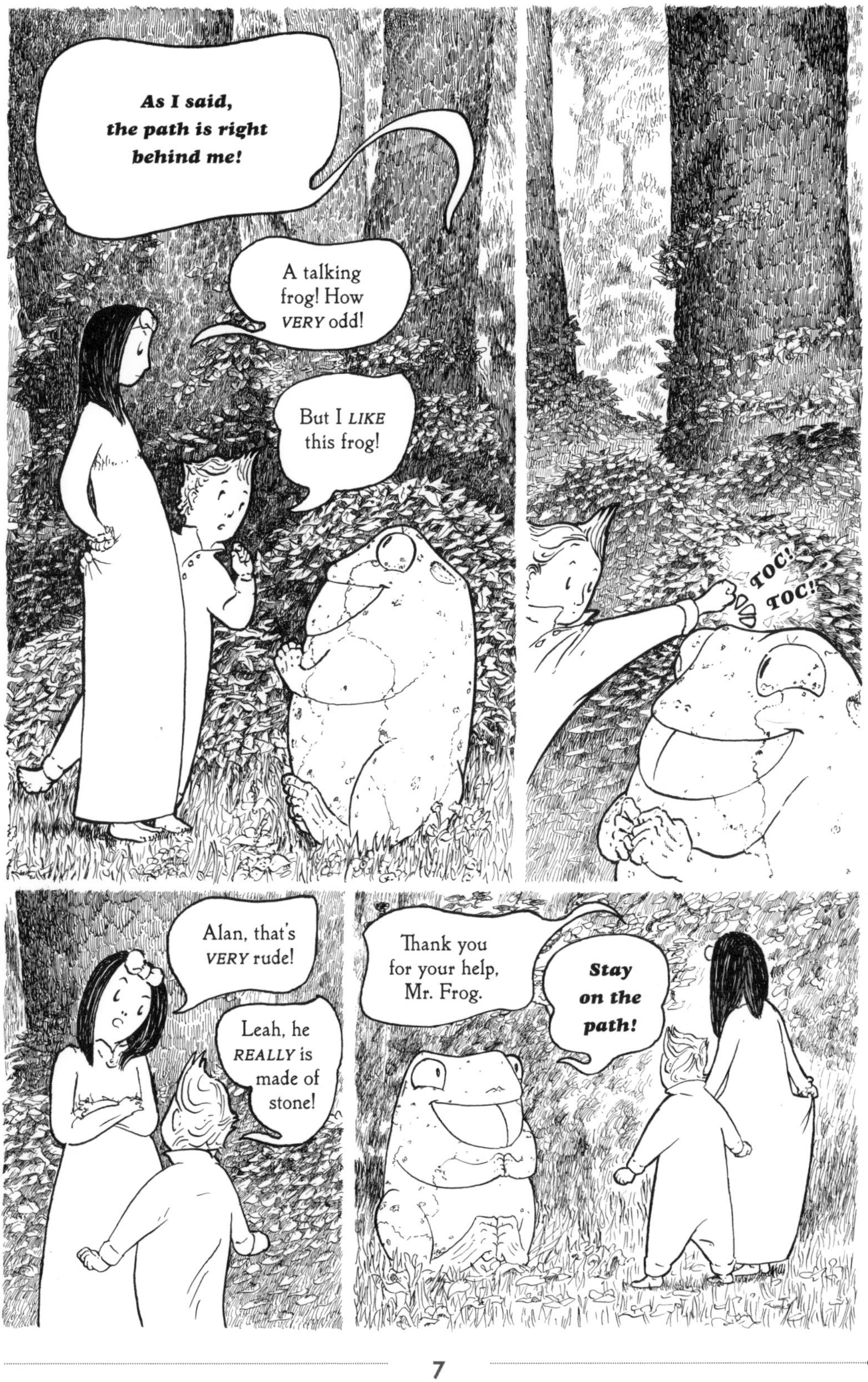

As I said, the path is right behind me!
A talking frog! How VERY odd!
But I LIKE this frog!
TOC! TOC!
Alan, that's VERY rude!
Leah, he REALLY is made of stone!
Thank you for your help, Mr. Frog.
Stay on the path!

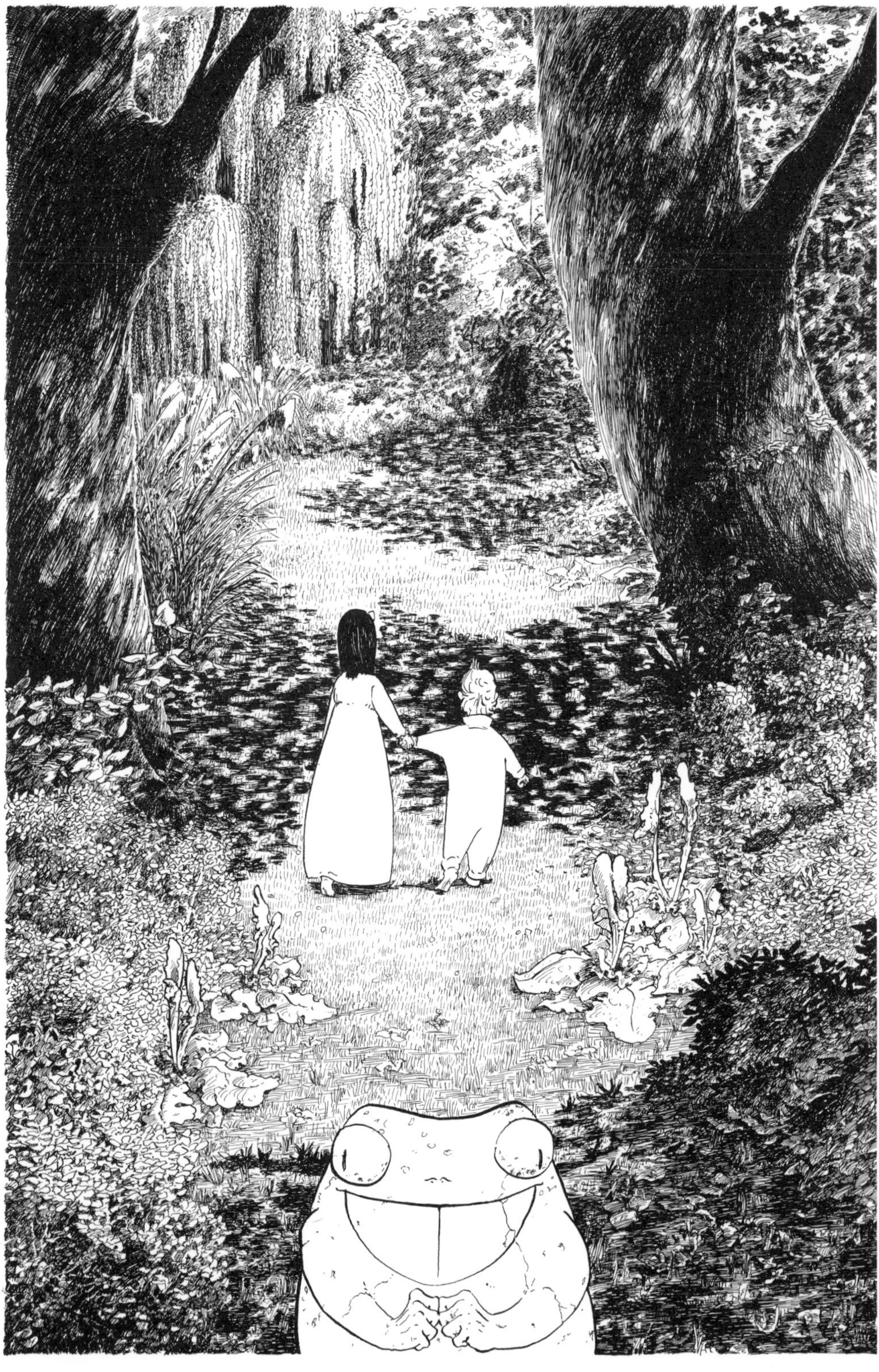

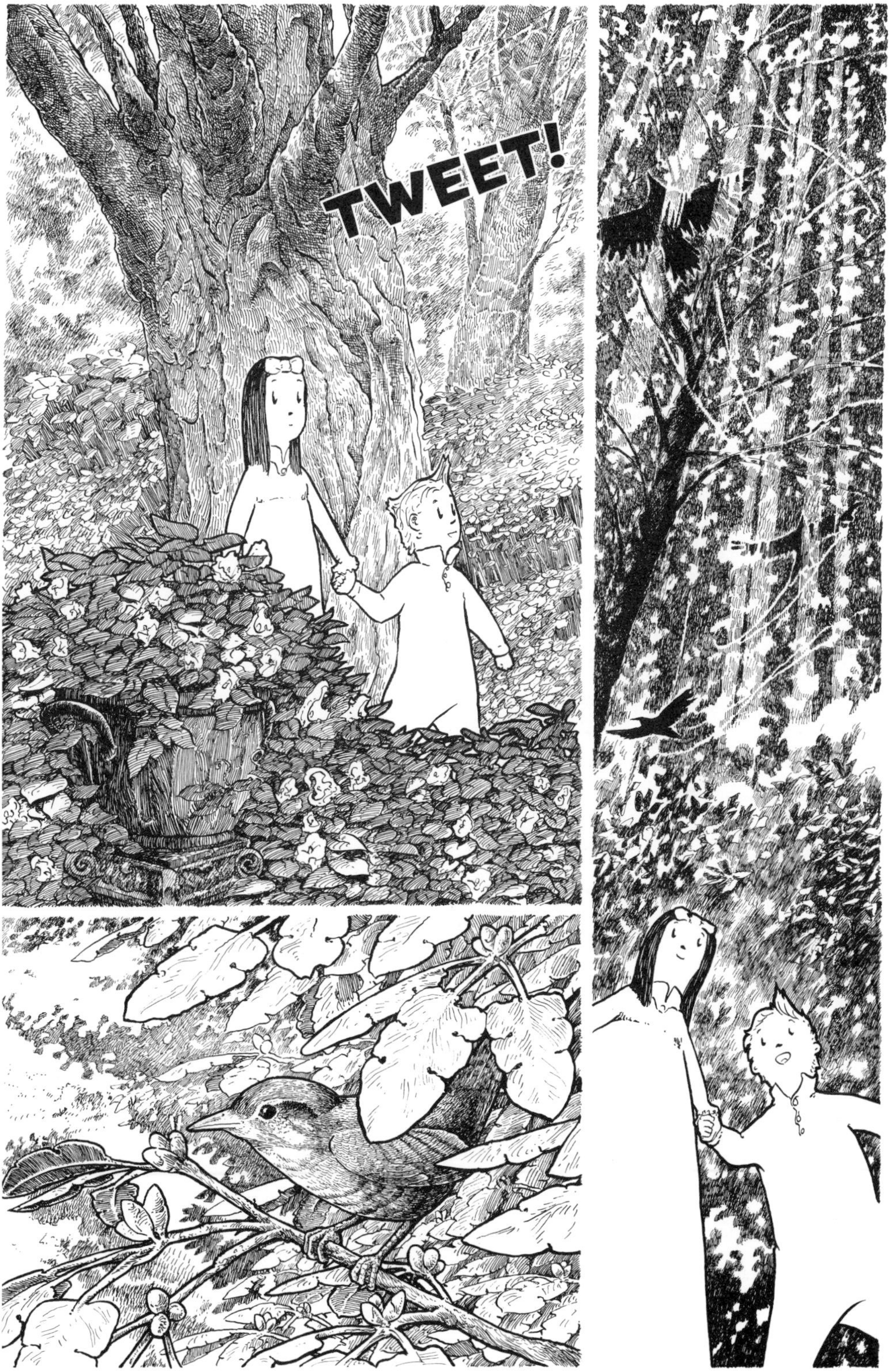
TWEET!

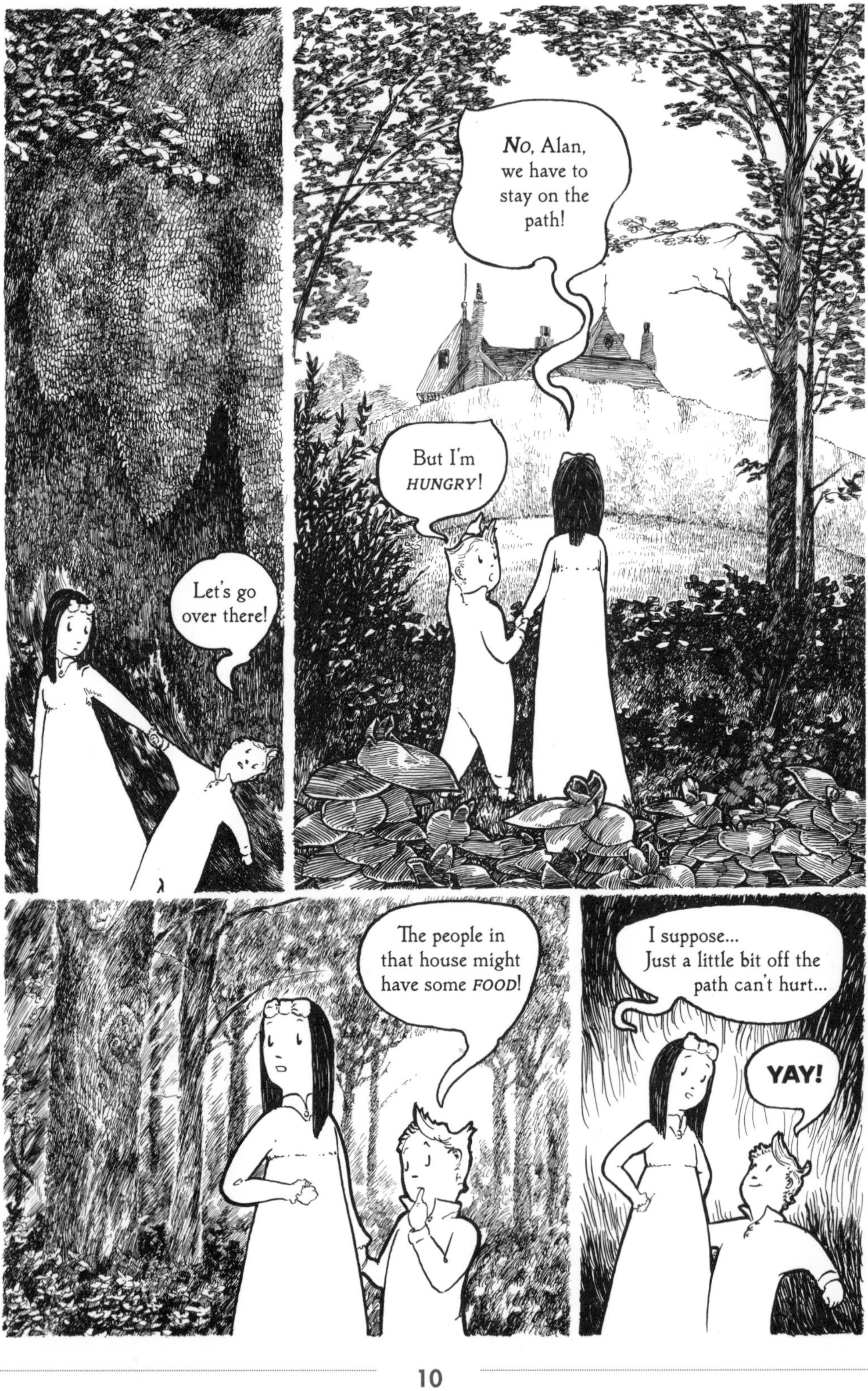
Let's go over there!
NO, Alan, we have to stay on the path!
But I'm HUNGRY!
The people in that house might have some FOOD!
I suppose... Just a little bit off the path can't hurt...
YAY!

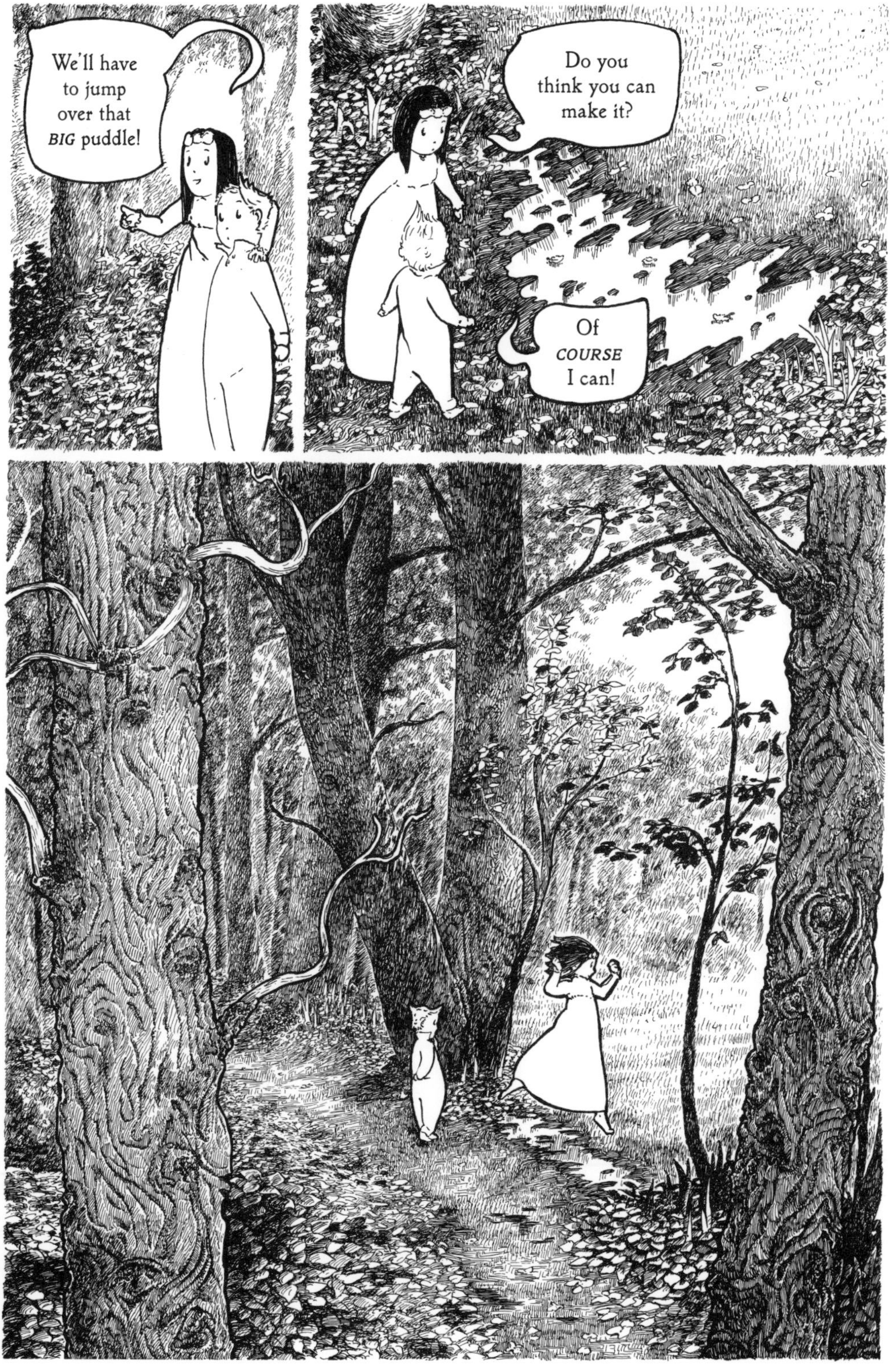
We'll have to jump over that *BIG* puddle!
Do you think you can make it?
Of *COURSE* I can!

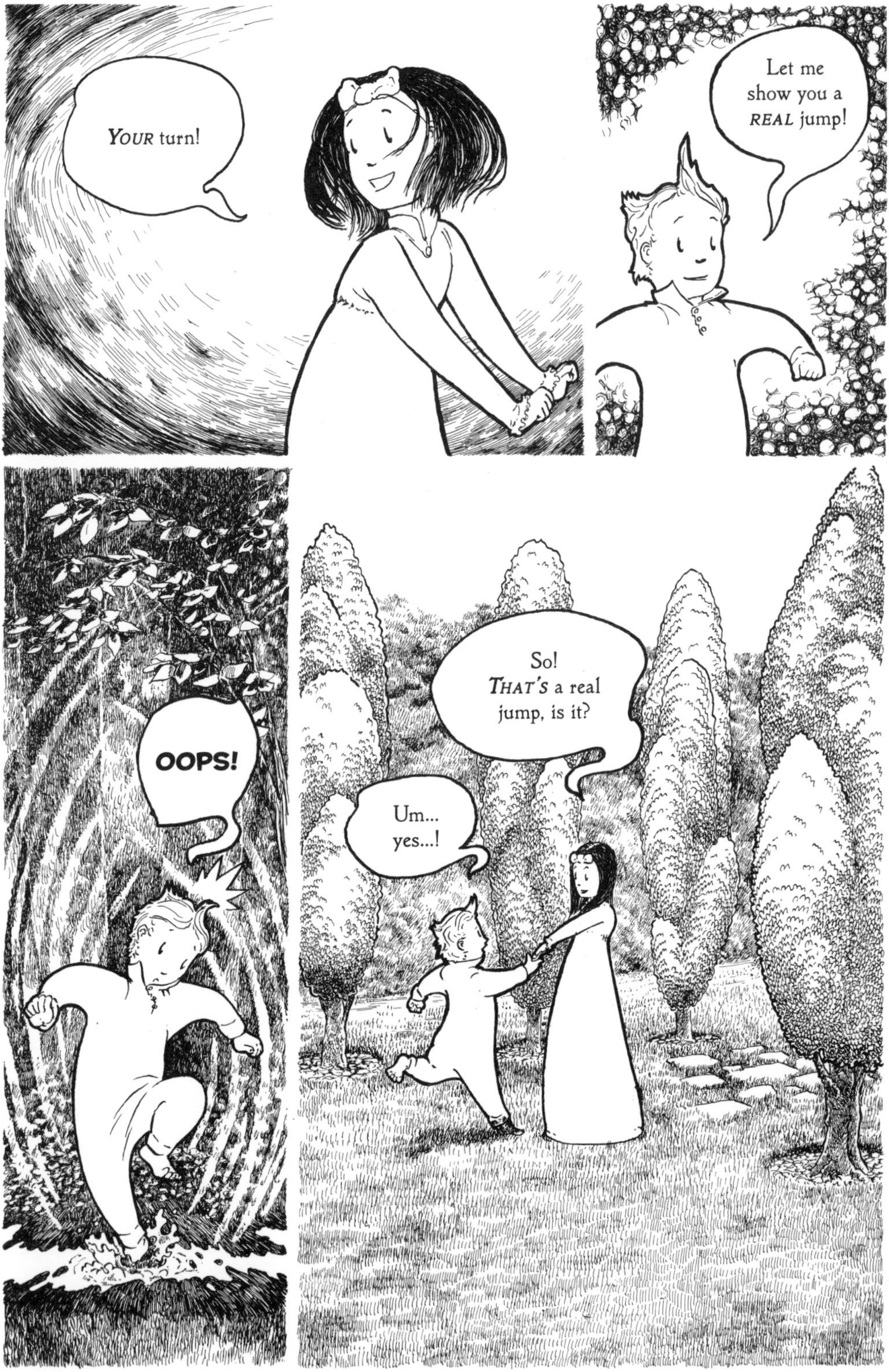
YOUR turn!
Let me show you a *REAL* jump!
OOPS!
So! *THAT'S* a real jump, is it?
Um... yes...!

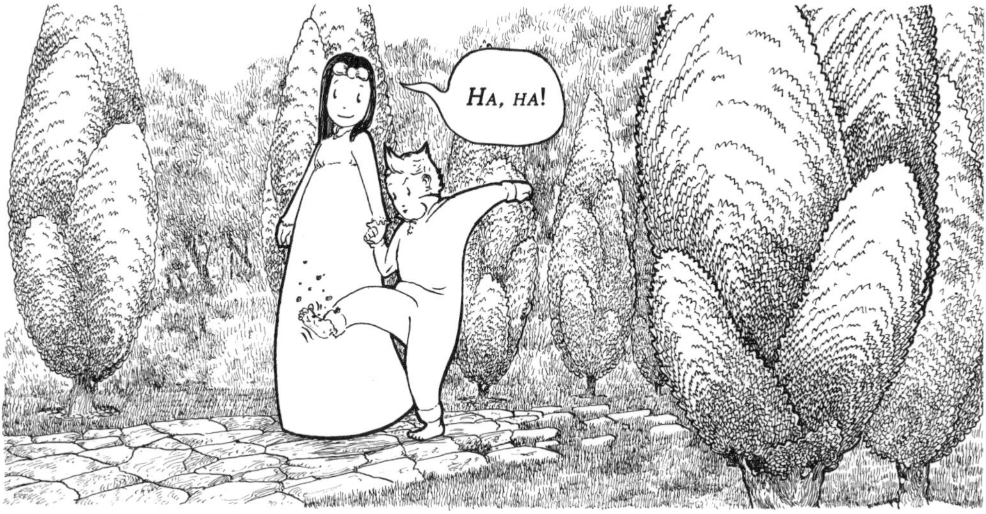
HA, HA!

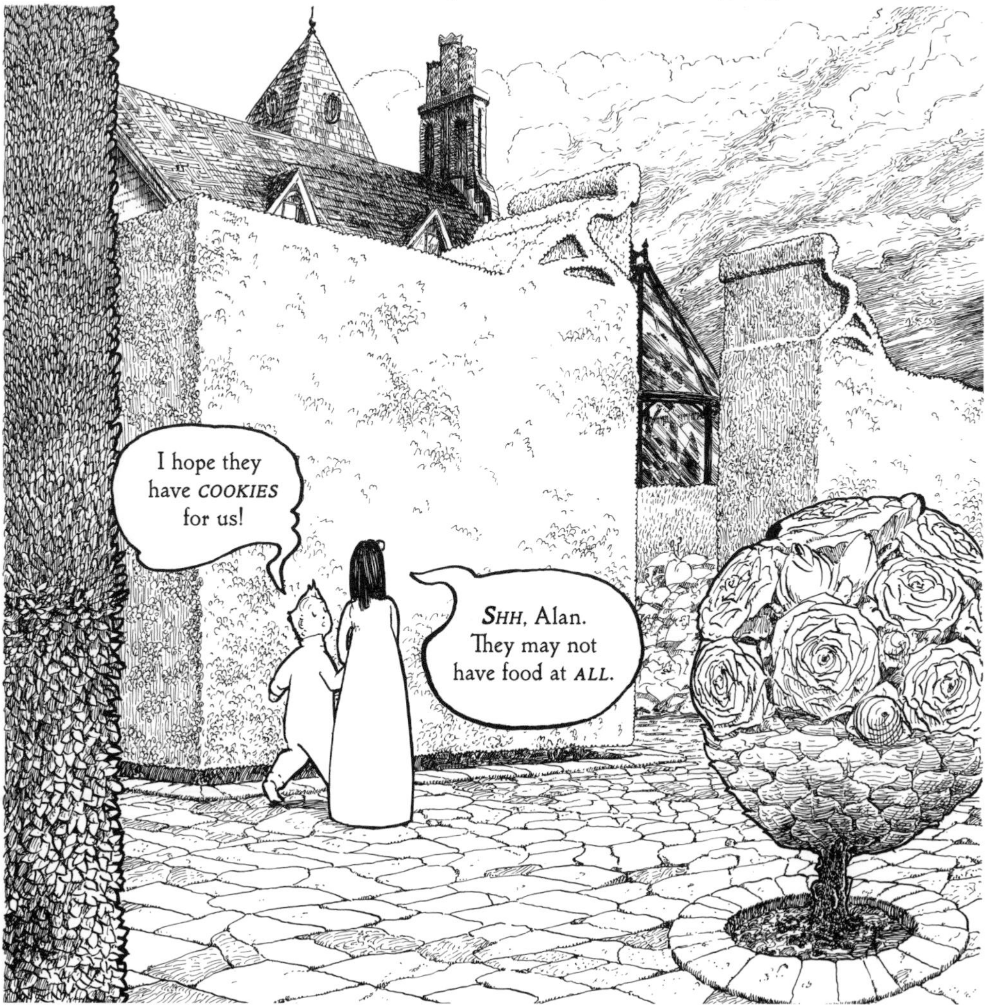
I hope they have COOKIES for us!
SHH, Alan. They may not have food at ALL.

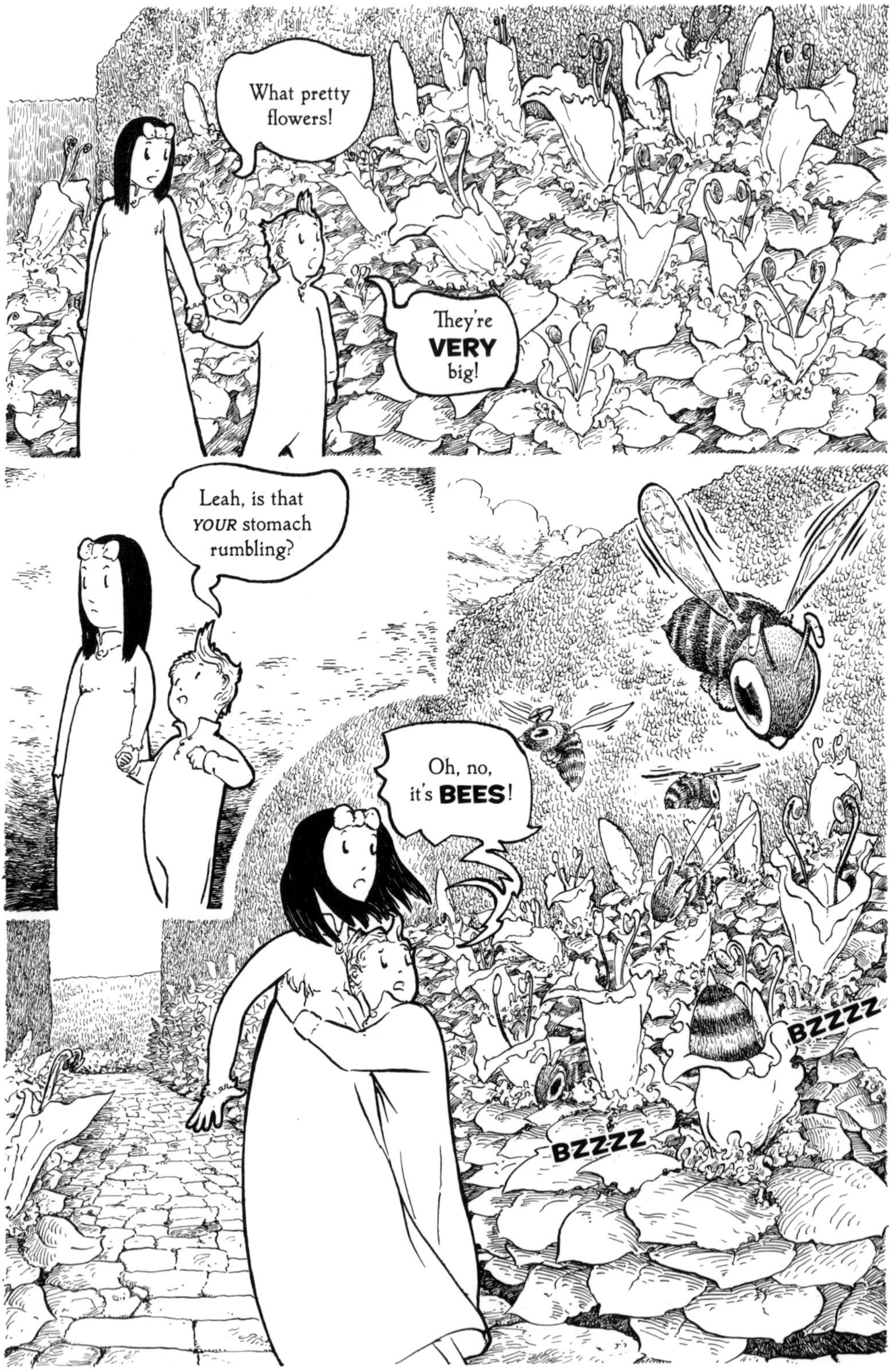
What pretty flowers!
They're VERY big!
Leah, is that YOUR stomach rumbling?
Oh, no, it's BEES!
BZZZZ
BZZZZ

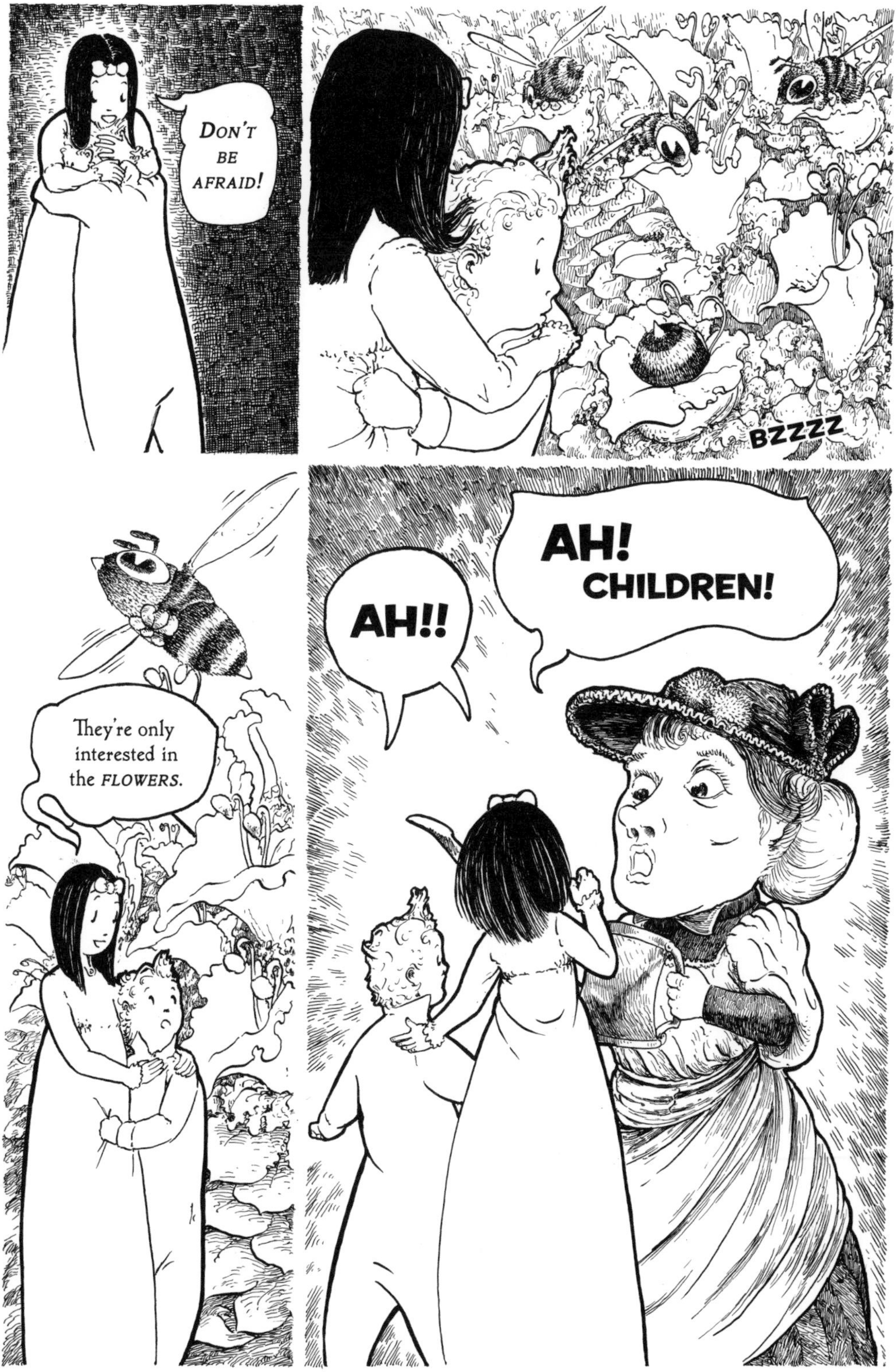
DON'T BE AFRAID!
BZZZZ
They're only interested in the *FLOWERS*.
AH!!
AH! CHILDREN!

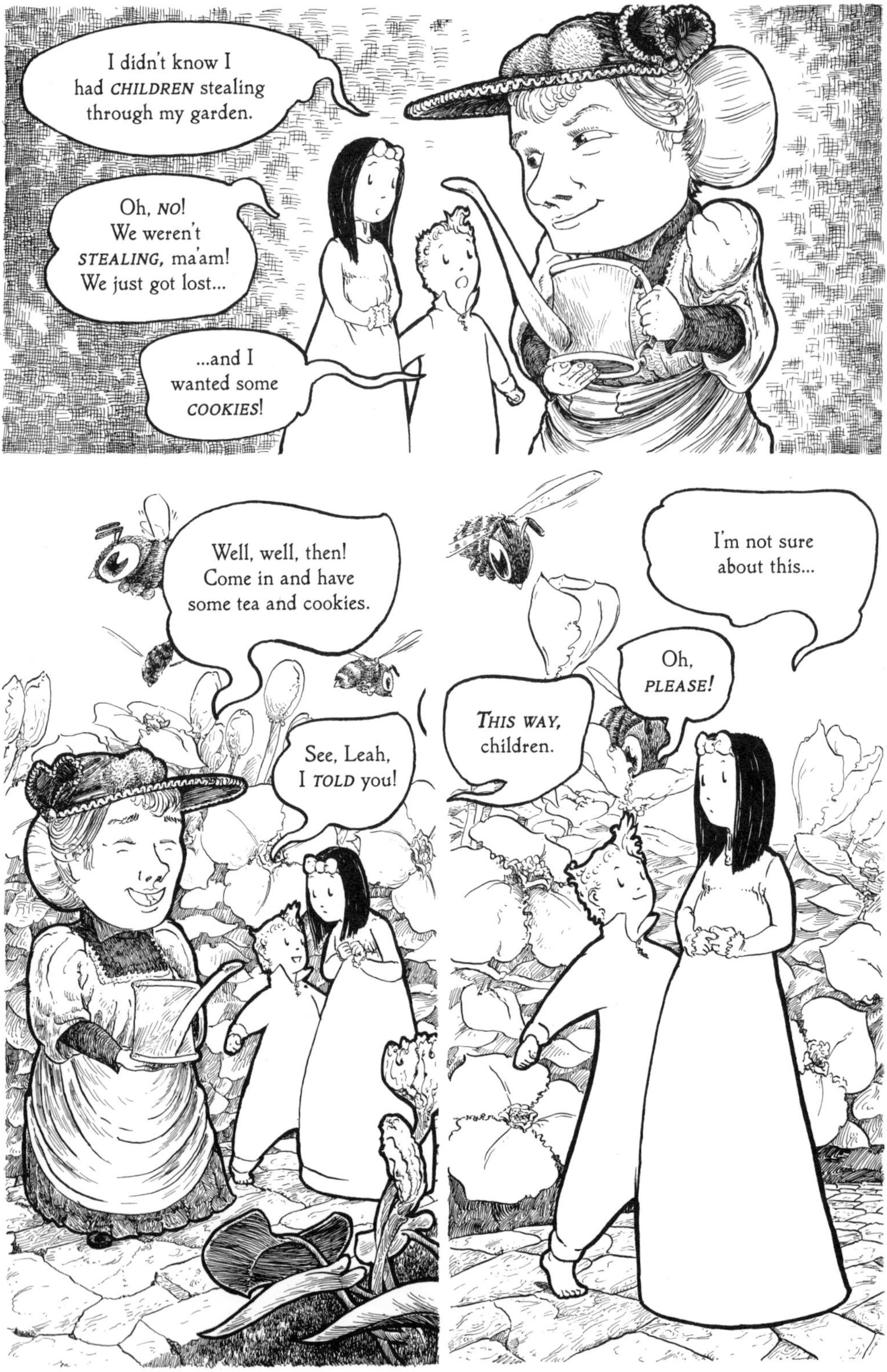
I didn't know I had CHILDREN stealing through my garden.
Oh, NO! We weren't STEALING, ma'am! We just got lost...
...and I wanted some COOKIES!
Well, well, then! Come in and have some tea and cookies.
See, Leah, I TOLD you!
I'm not sure about this...
Oh, PLEASE!
THIS WAY, children.

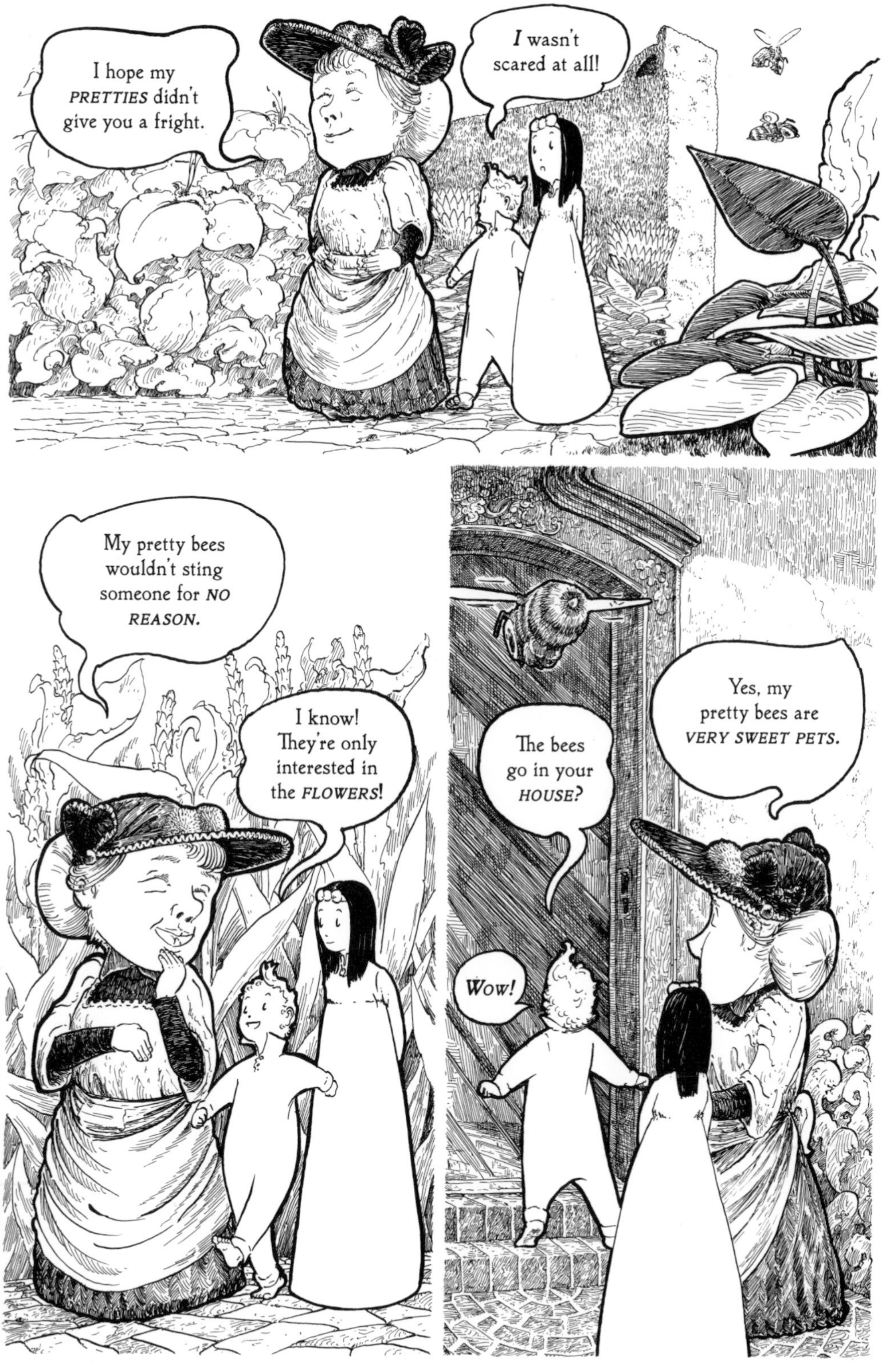

I hope my PRETTIES didn't give you a fright.
I wasn't scared at all!
My pretty bees wouldn't sting someone for NO REASON.
I know! They're only interested in the FLOWERS!
The bees go in your HOUSE?
Yes, my pretty bees are VERY SWEET PETS.
Wow!

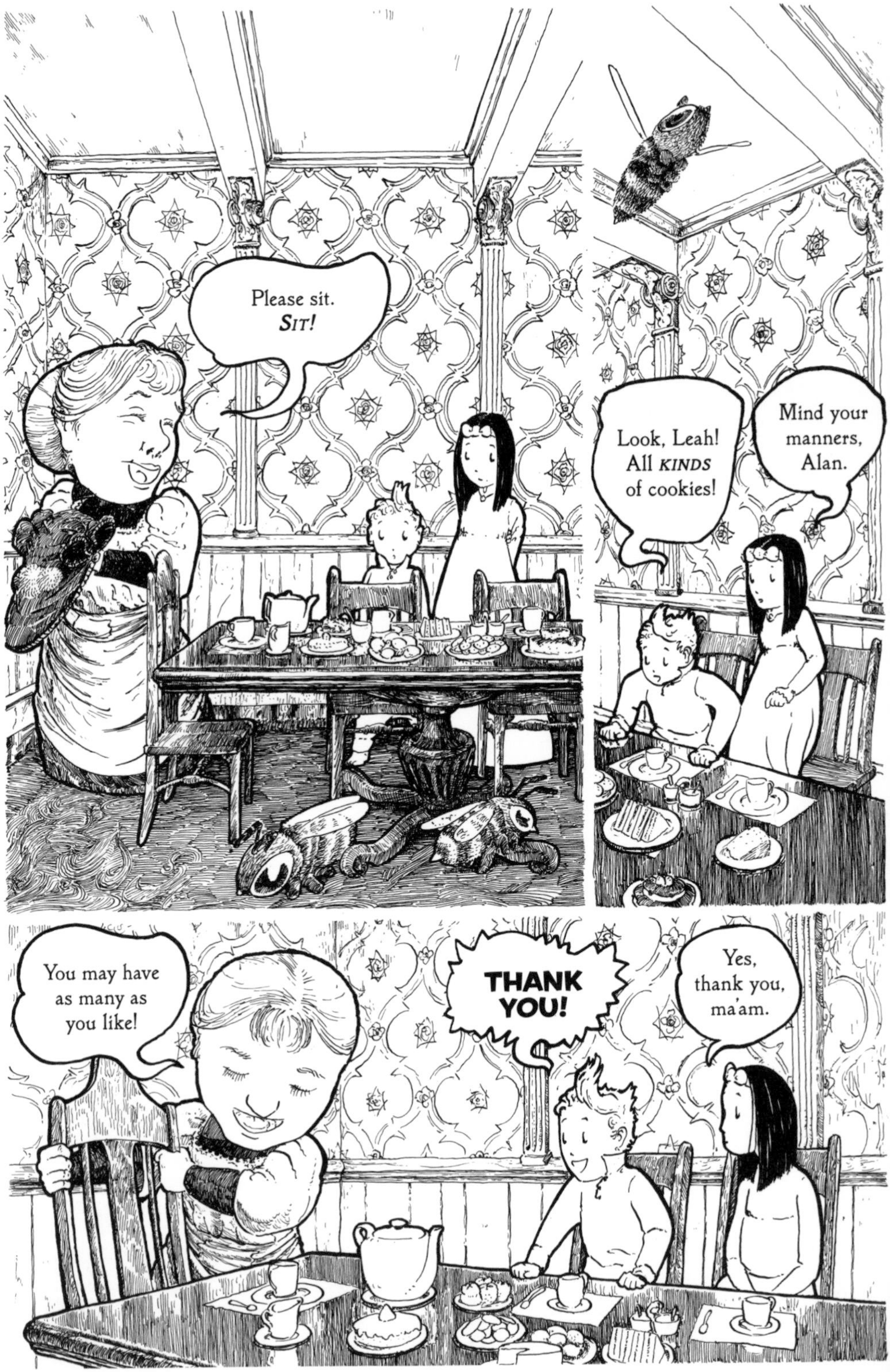
Please sit.
SIT!
Look, Leah! All *KINDS* of cookies!
Mind your manners, Alan.
You may have as many as you like!
THANK YOU!
Yes, thank you, ma'am.

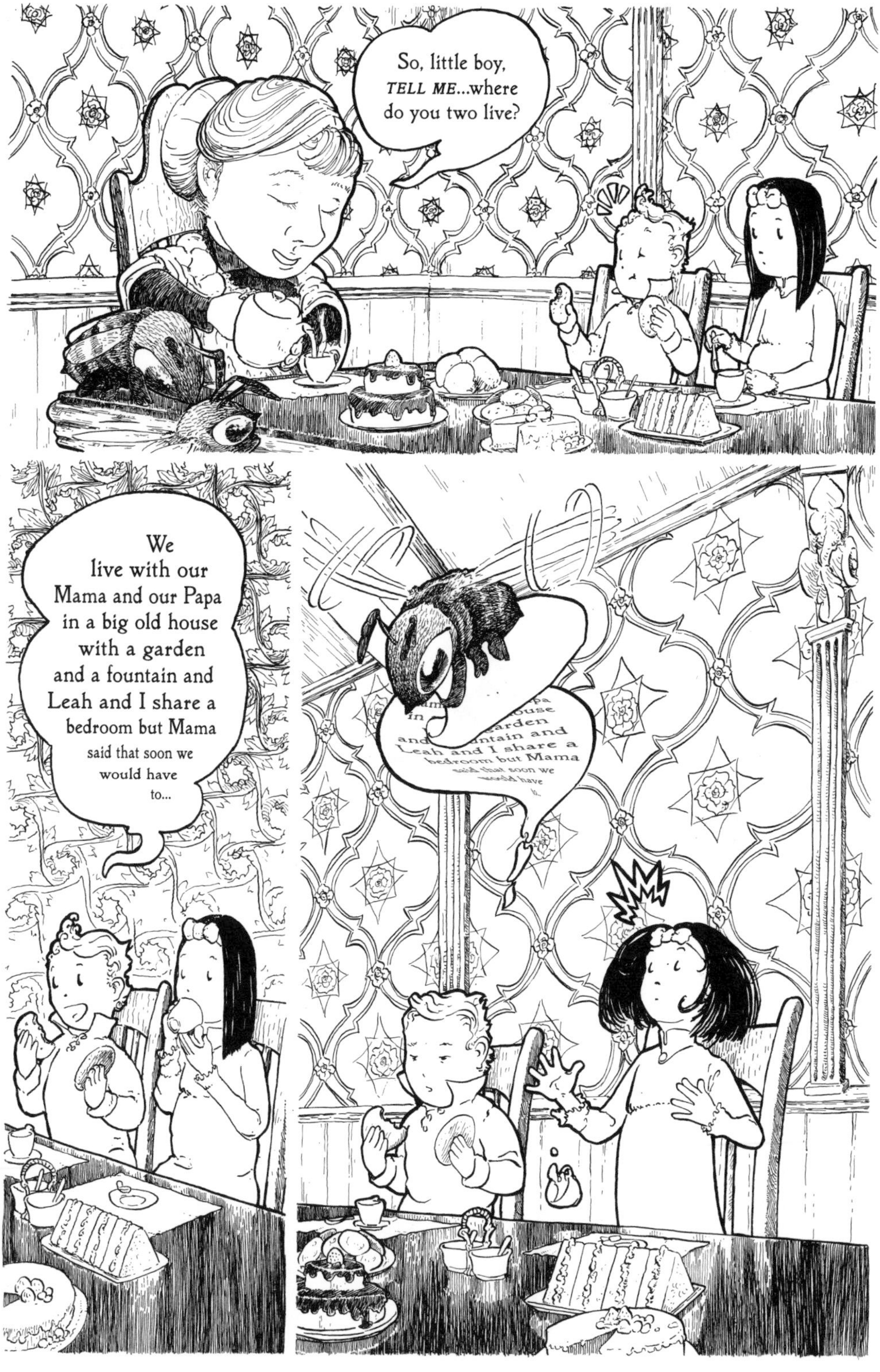

So, little boy, *TELL ME*...where do you two live?
We live with our Mama and our Papa in a big old house with a garden and a fountain and Leah and I share a bedroom but Mama said that soon we would have to...
Leah and I share a
bedroom but Mama
said that soon we
would have

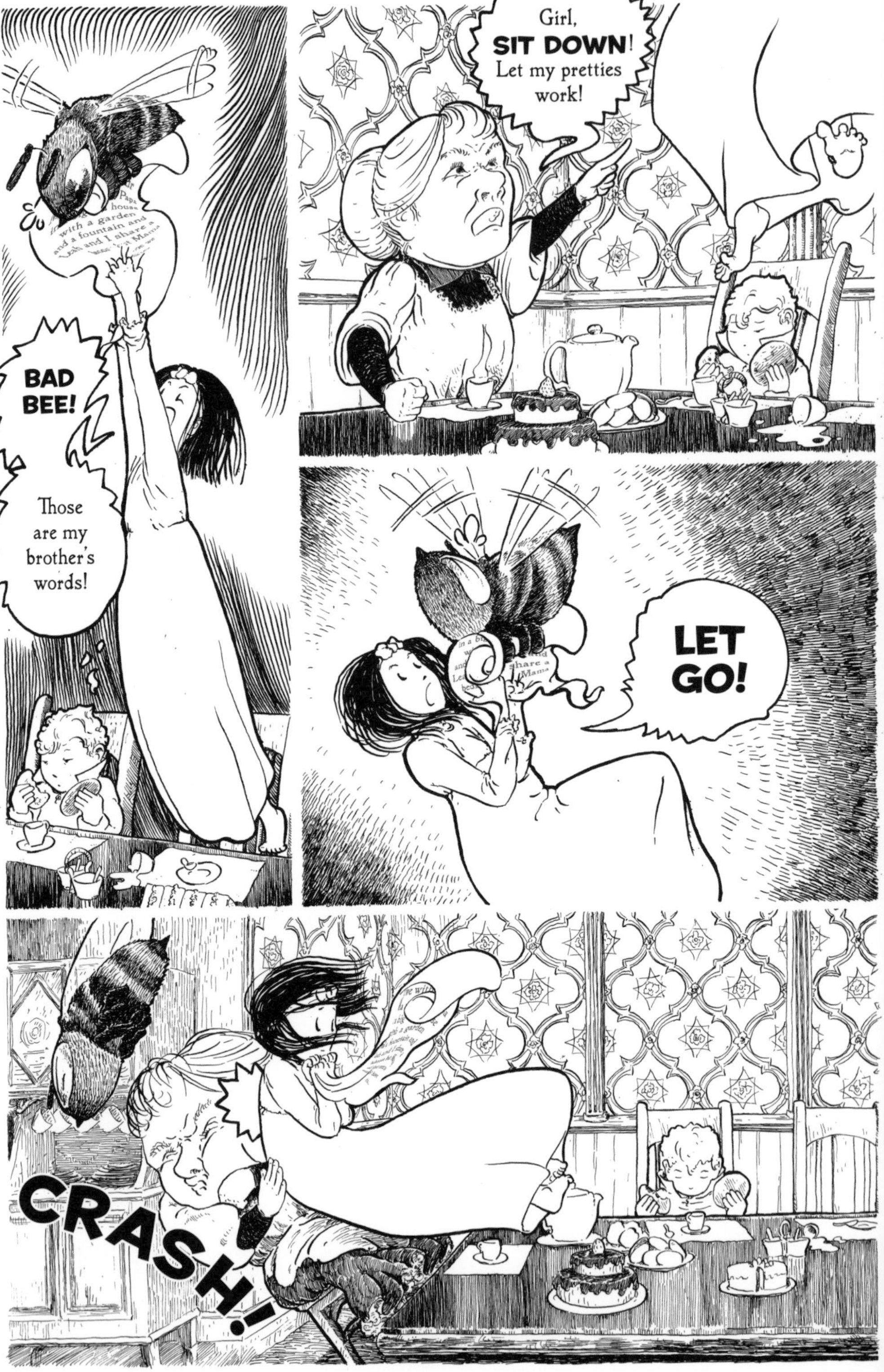
BAD BEE!
Those are my brother's words!
Girl, SIT DOWN! Let my pretties work!
LET GO!
CRASH!

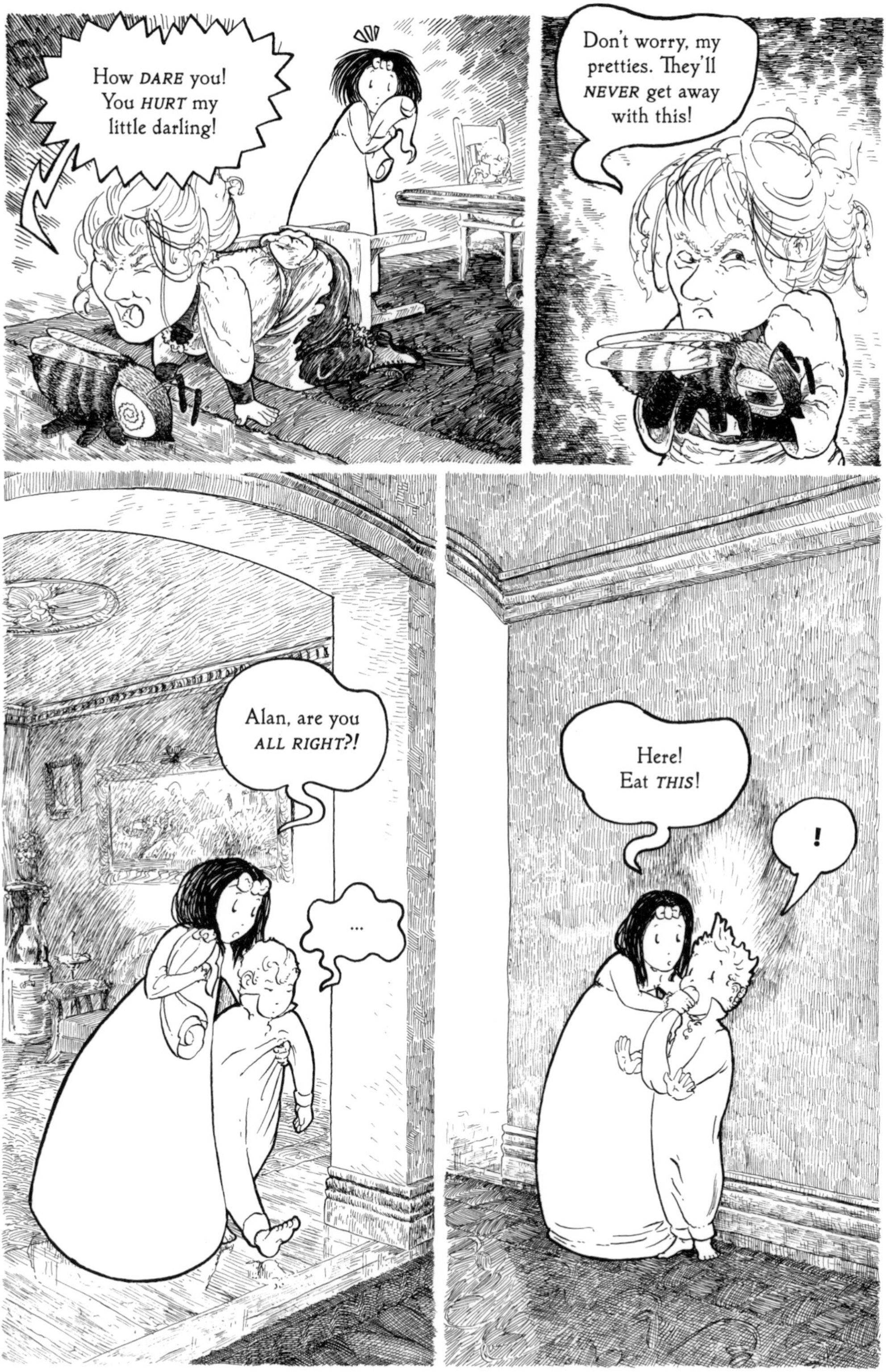
How *DARE* you! You *HURT* my little darling!
Don't worry, my pretties. They'll *NEVER* get away with this!
Alan, are you *ALL RIGHT*?!
...
Here! Eat *THIS*!
!

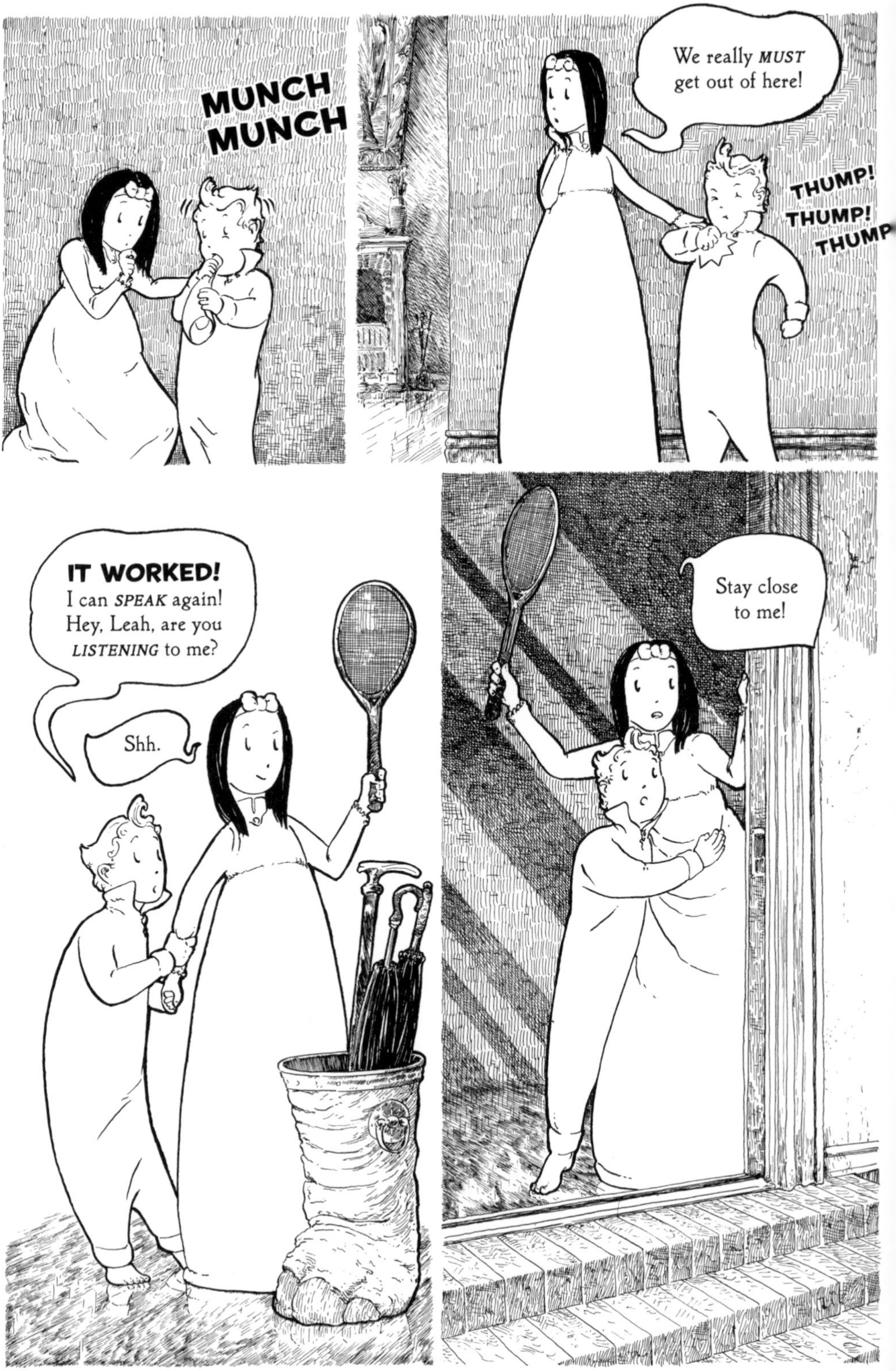
MUNCH MUNCH
We really MUST get out of here!
THUMP! THUMP! THUMP
IT WORKED! I can SPEAK again! Hey, Leah, are you LISTENING to me?
Shh.
Stay close to me!

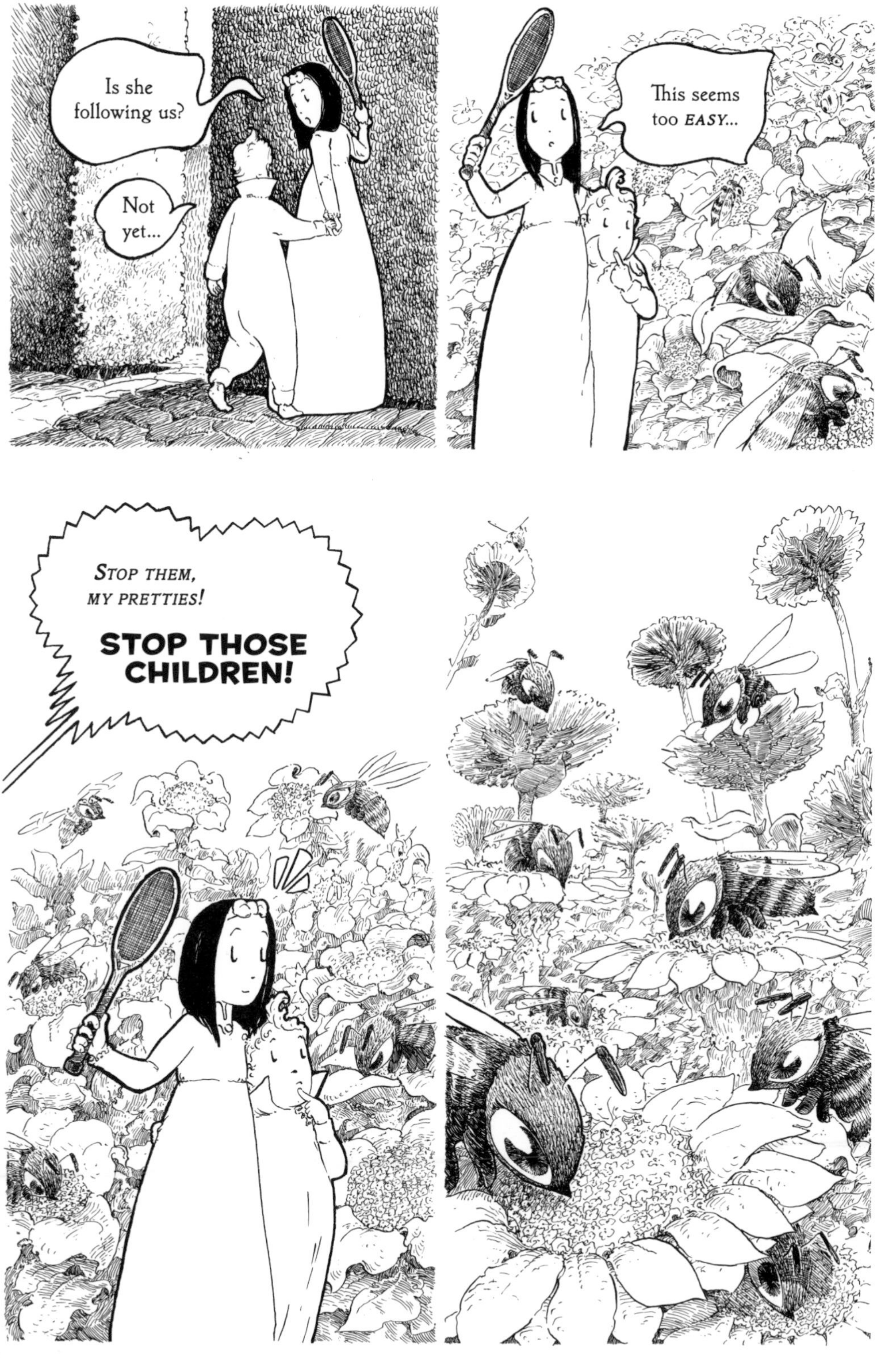

Is she following us?
Not yet...
This seems too EASY...
STOP THEM, MY PRETTIES!
STOP THOSE CHILDREN!

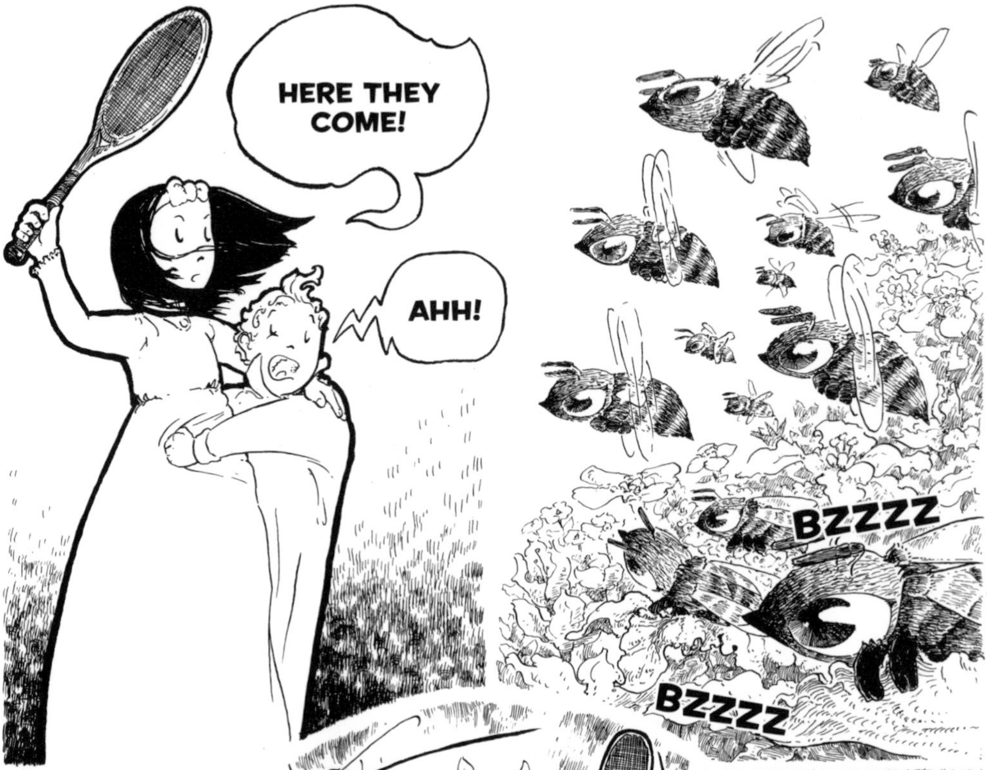
HERE THEY COME!
AHH!
BZZZZ
BZZZZ

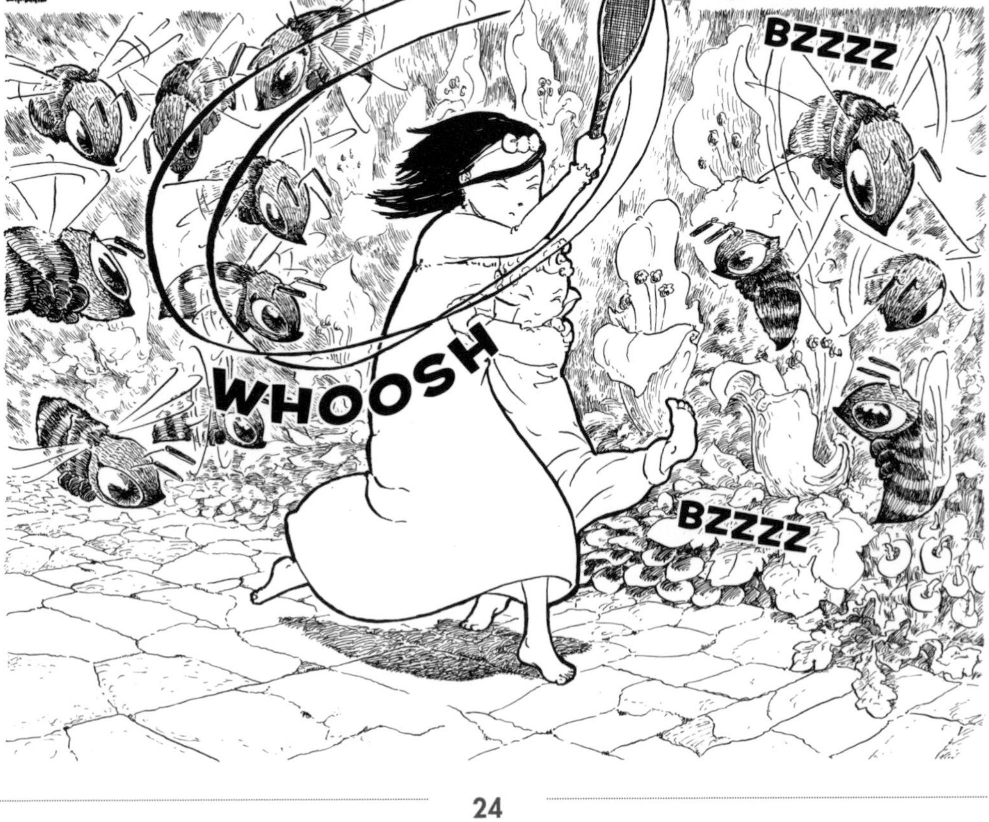
BZZZZ
WHOOSH
BZZZZ

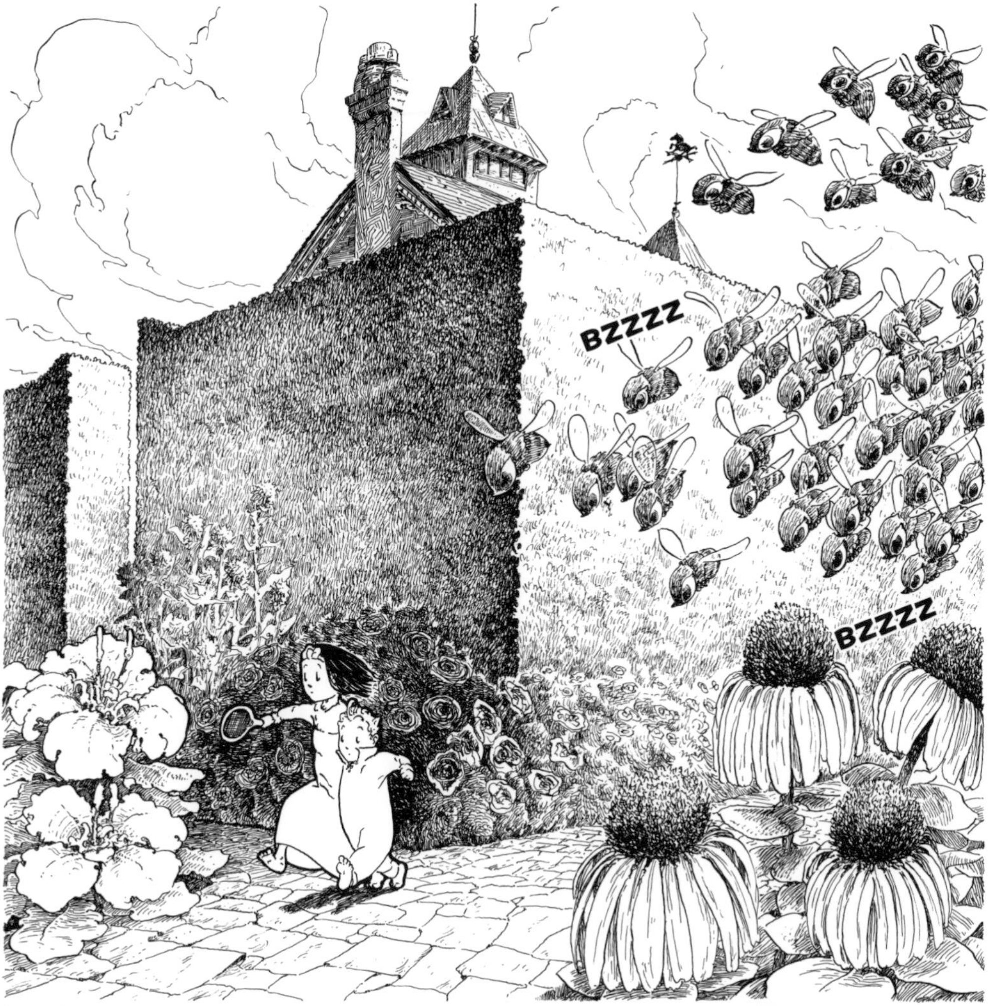
BZZZZ
BZZZZ

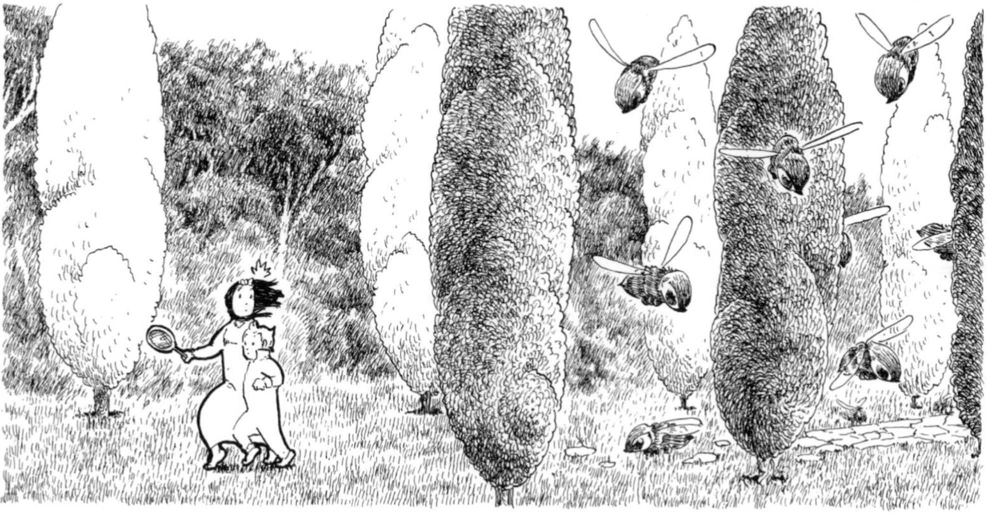

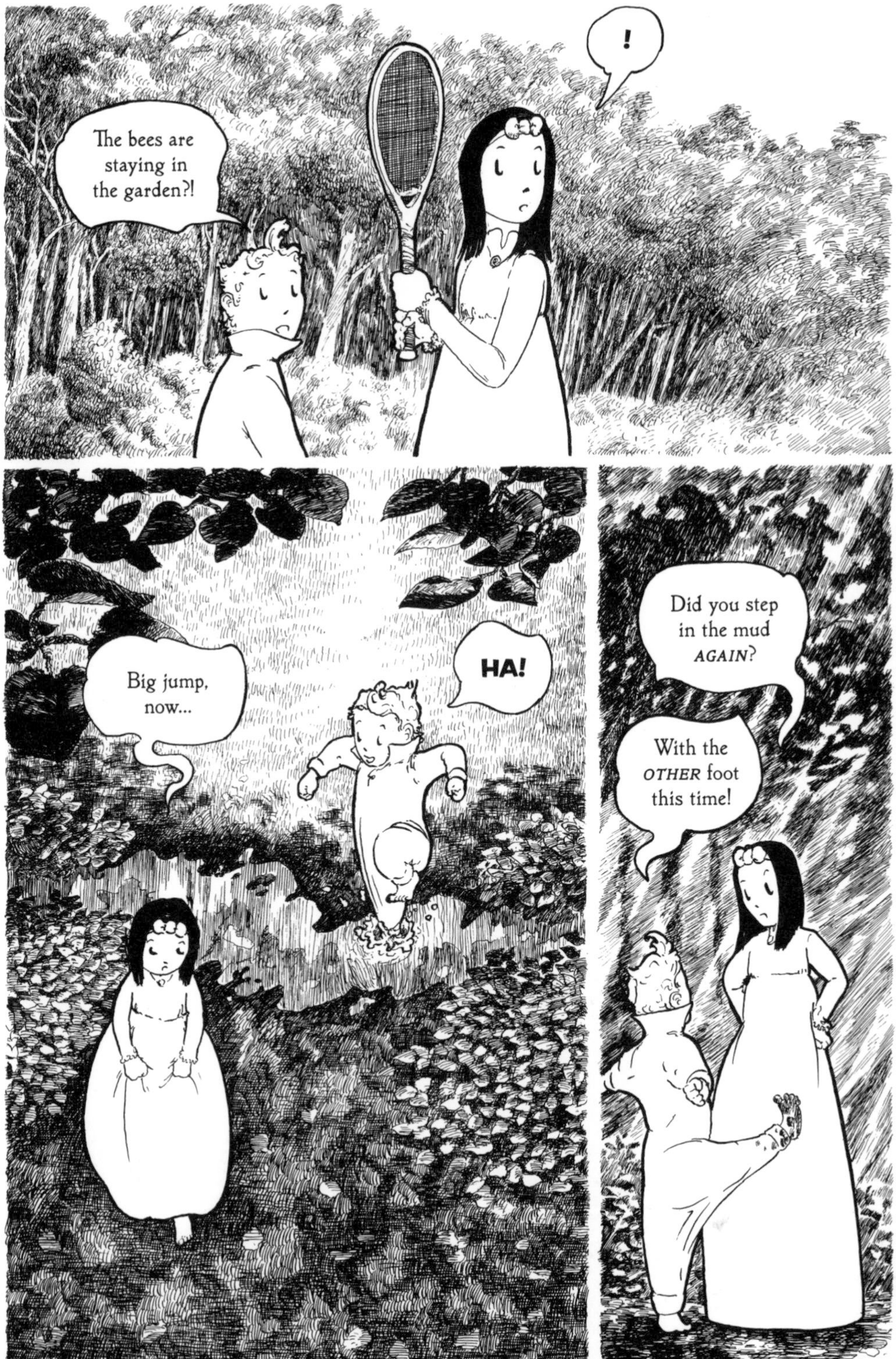
The bees are staying in the garden?!
!
Big jump, now...
HA!
Did you step in the mud AGAIN?
With the OTHER foot this time!

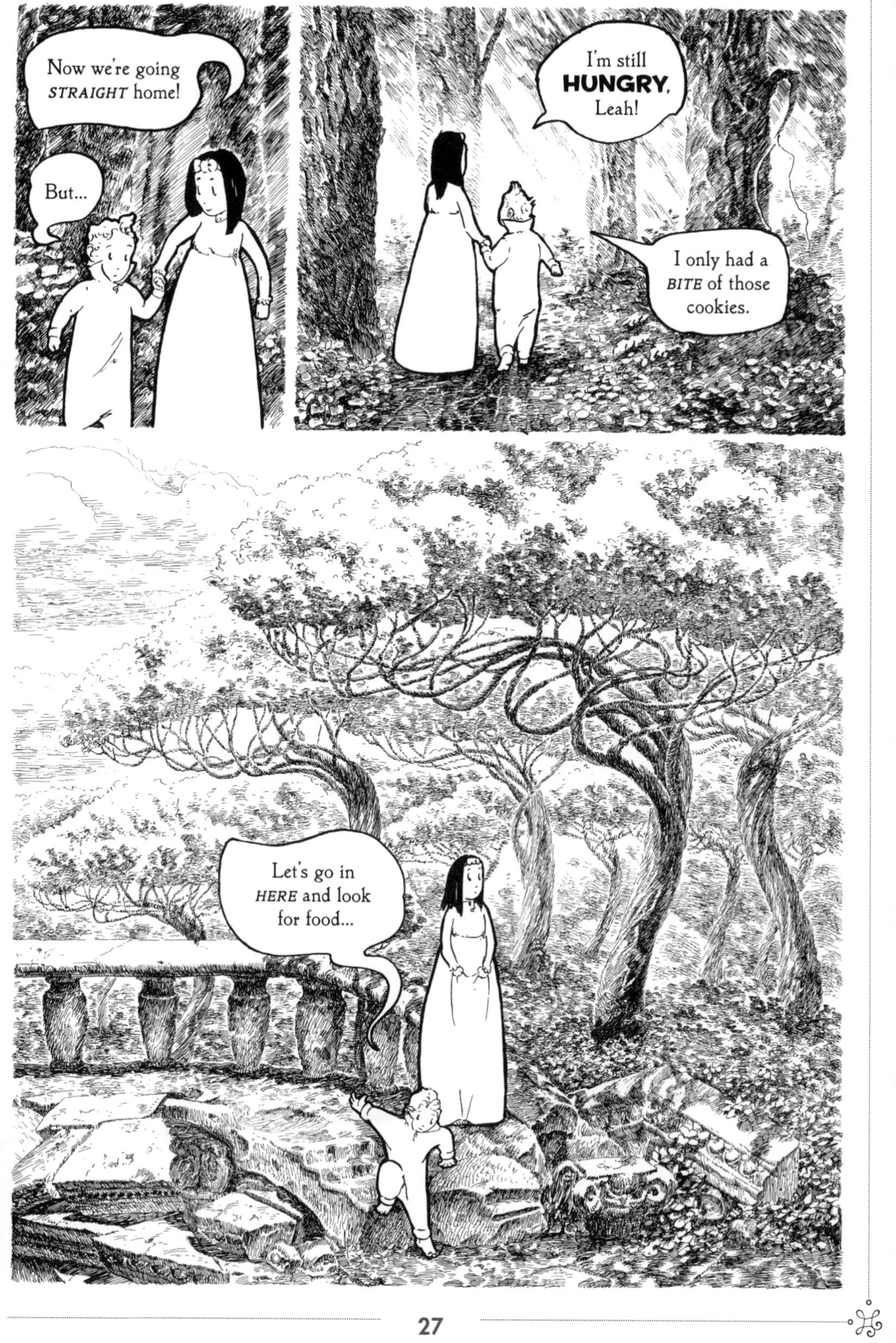
Now we're going *STRAIGHT* home!
But...
I'm still **HUNGRY**, Leah!
I only had a *BITE* of those cookies.
Let's go in *HERE* and look for food...

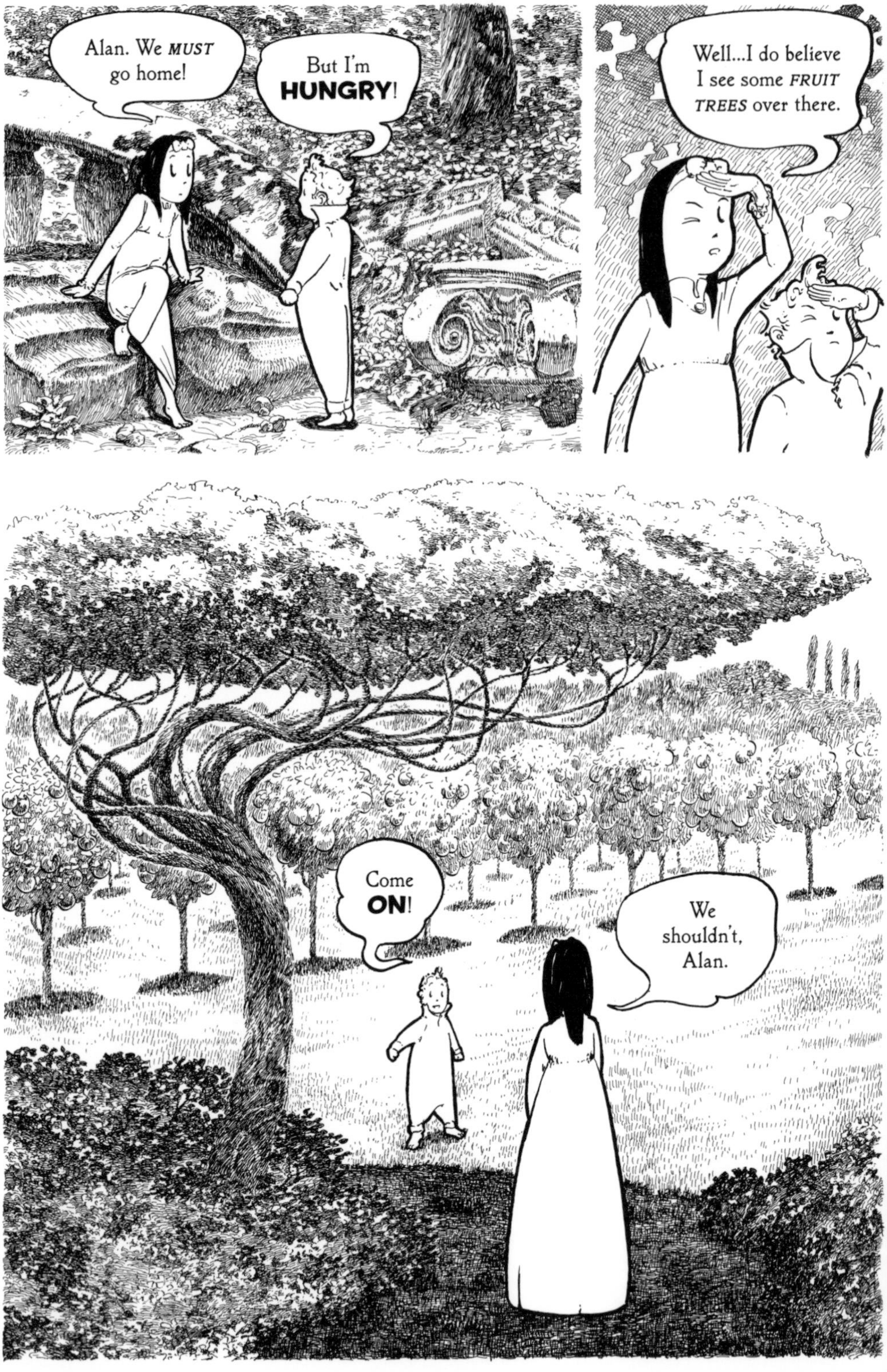
Alan. We *MUST* go home!
But I'm **HUNGRY**!
Well...I do believe I see some *FRUIT TREES* over there.
Come **ON**!
We shouldn't, Alan.

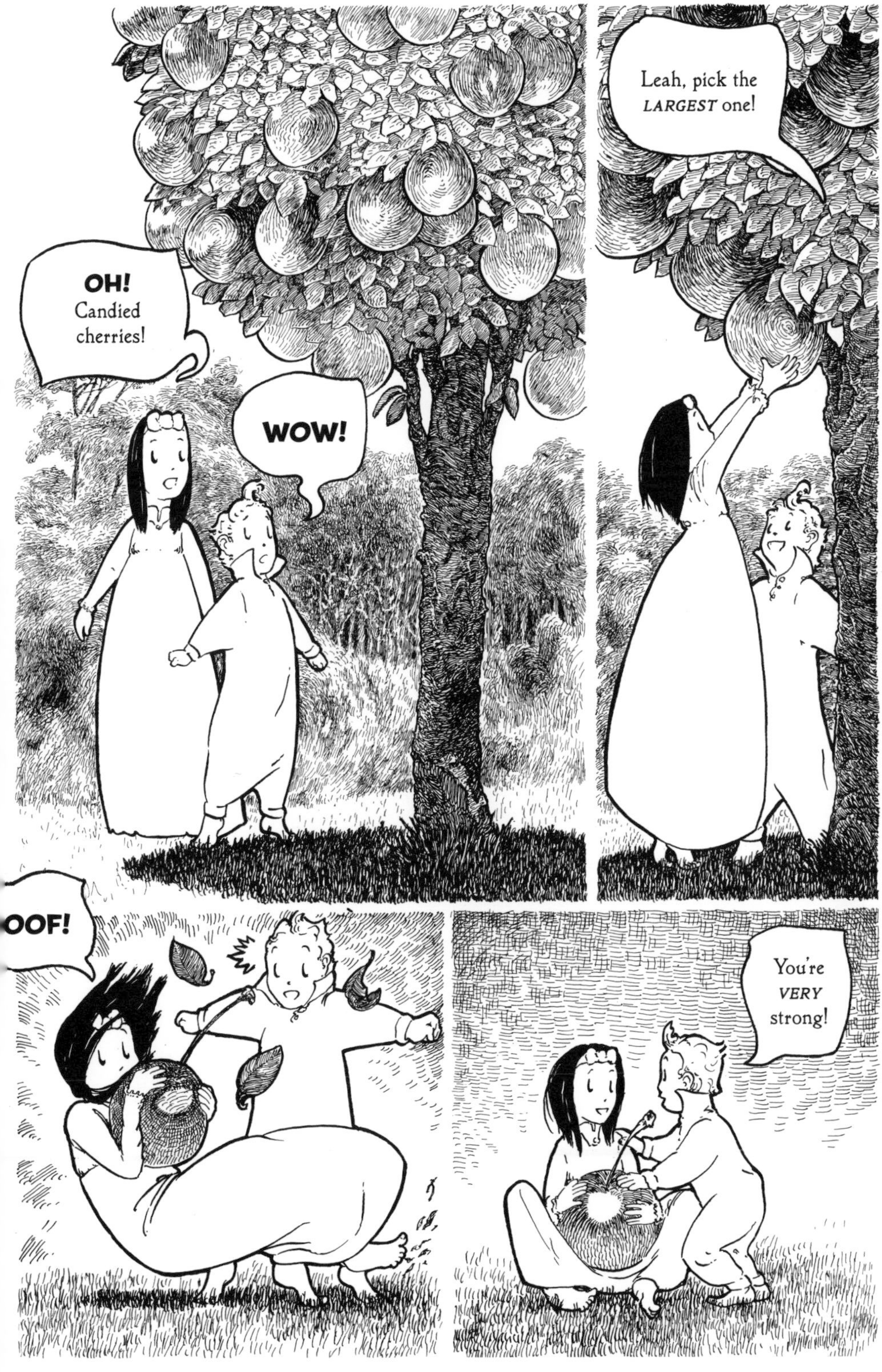
OH!
Candied cherries!
WOW!
Leah, pick the LARGEST one!
OOF!
You're VERY strong!

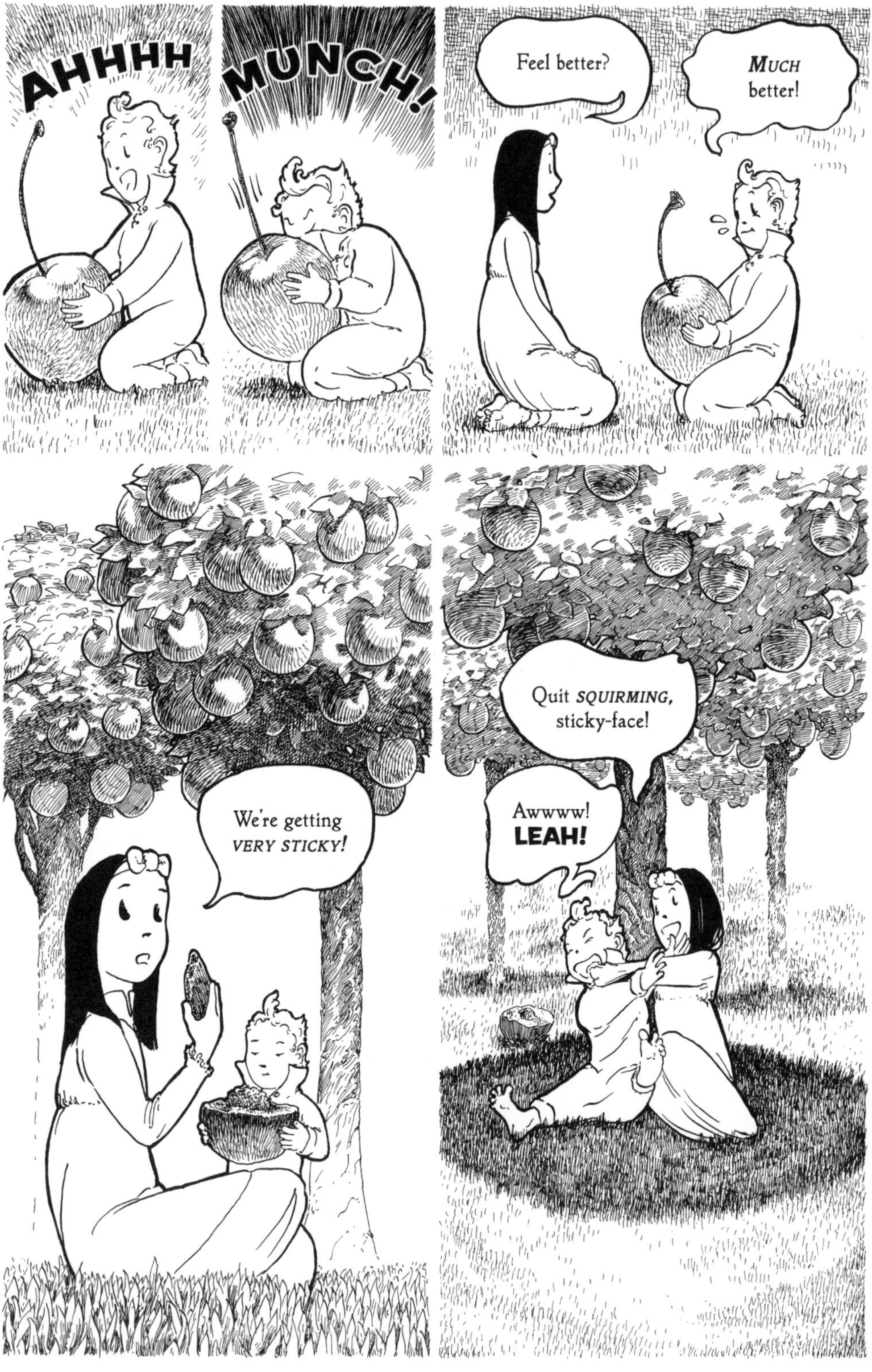

AHHHH
MUNCH!
Feel better?
MUCH better!
We're getting VERY STICKY!
Quit SQUIRMING, sticky-face!
Awwww! LEAH!

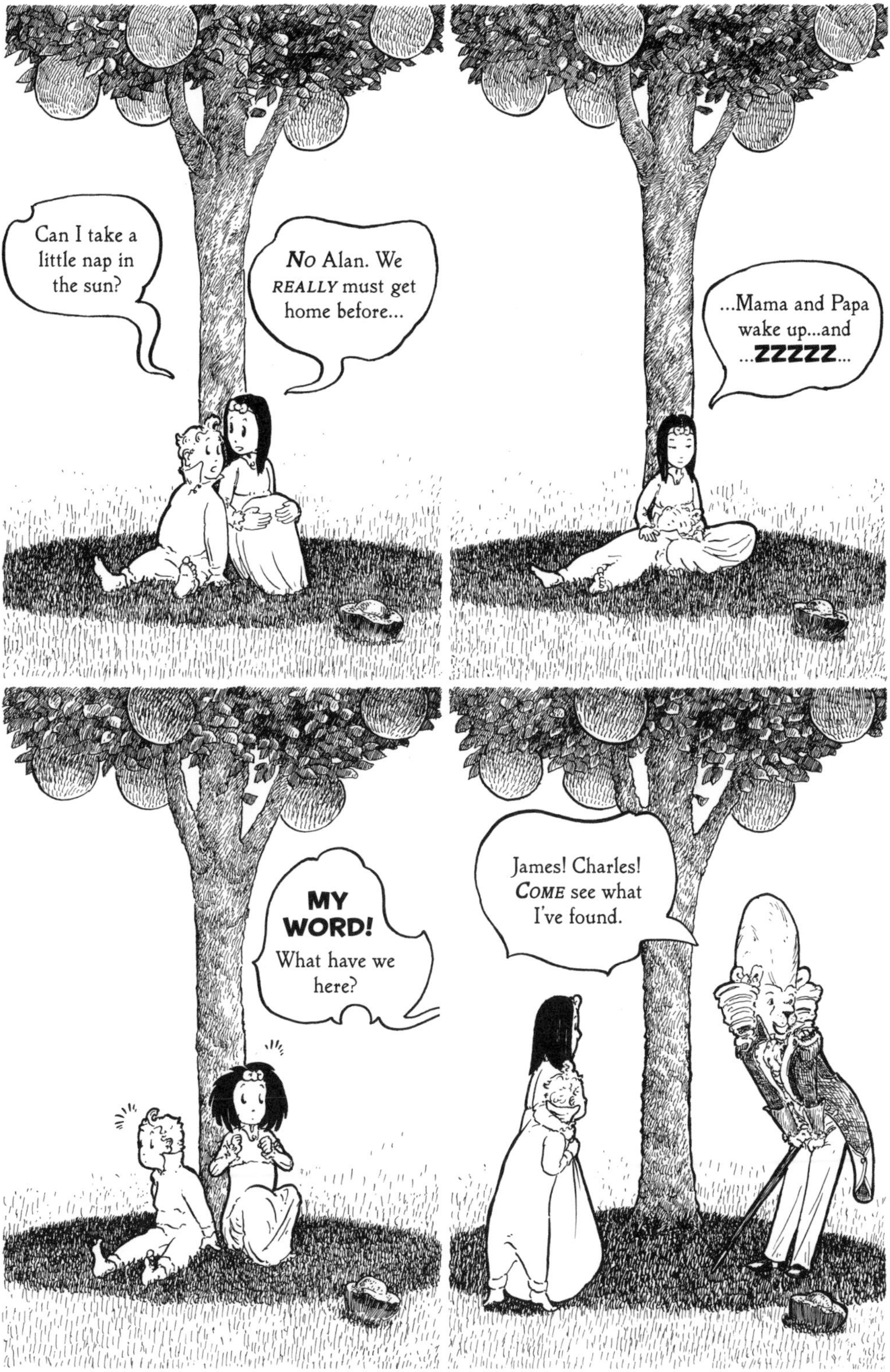
Can I take a little nap in the sun?
No Alan. We *REALLY* must get home before...
...Mama and Papa wake up...and ...**ZZZZZ**...
MY WORD! What have we here?
James! Charles! *COME* see what I've found.

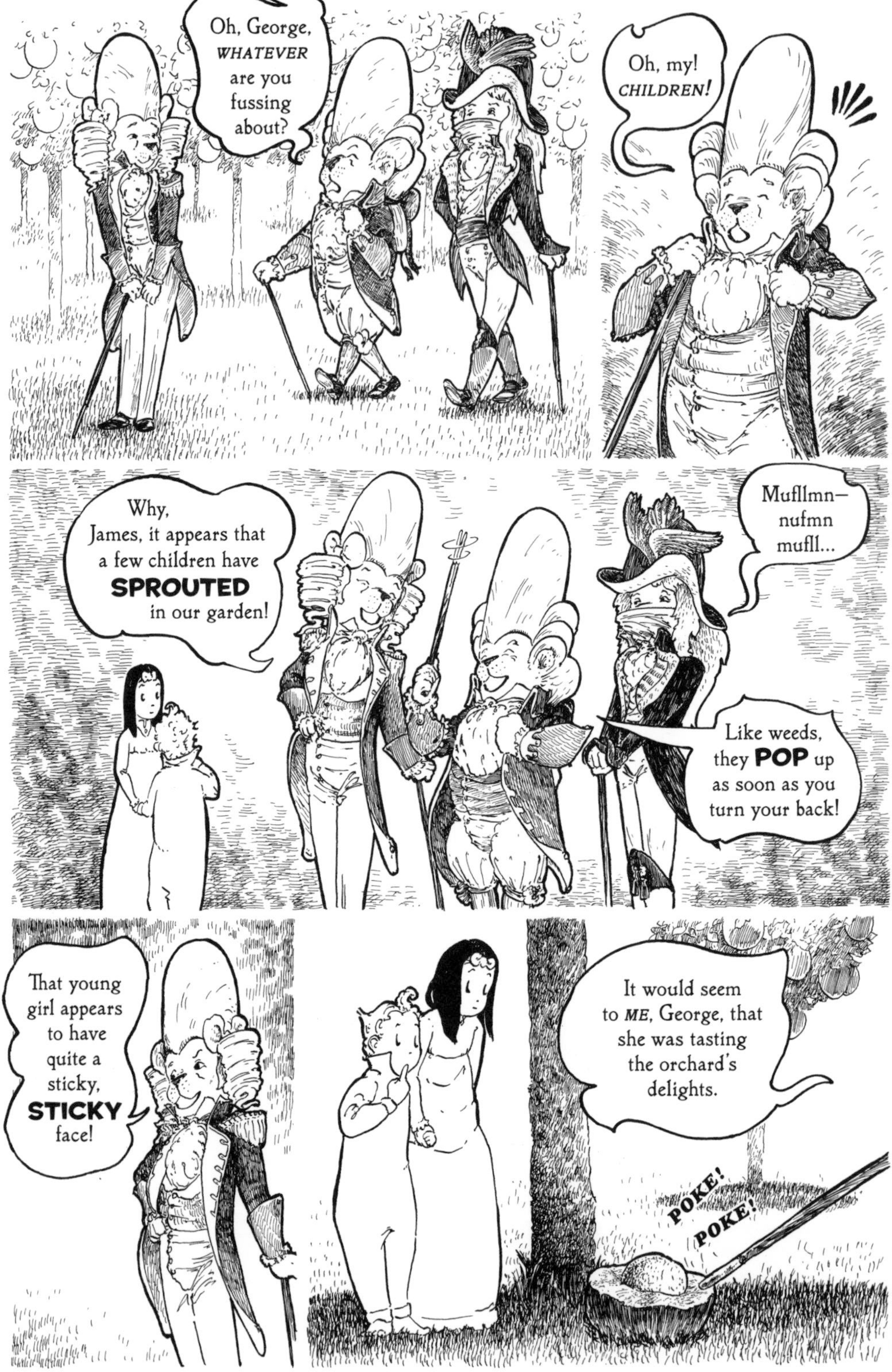

Oh, George, WHATEVER are you fussing about?
Oh, my! CHILDREN!
Why, James, it appears that a few children have SPROUTED in our garden!
Muflmn—nufmn mufll...
Like weeds, they POP up as soon as you turn your back!
That young girl appears to have quite a sticky, STICKY face!
It would seem to ME, George, that she was tasting the orchard's delights.
POKE! POKE!

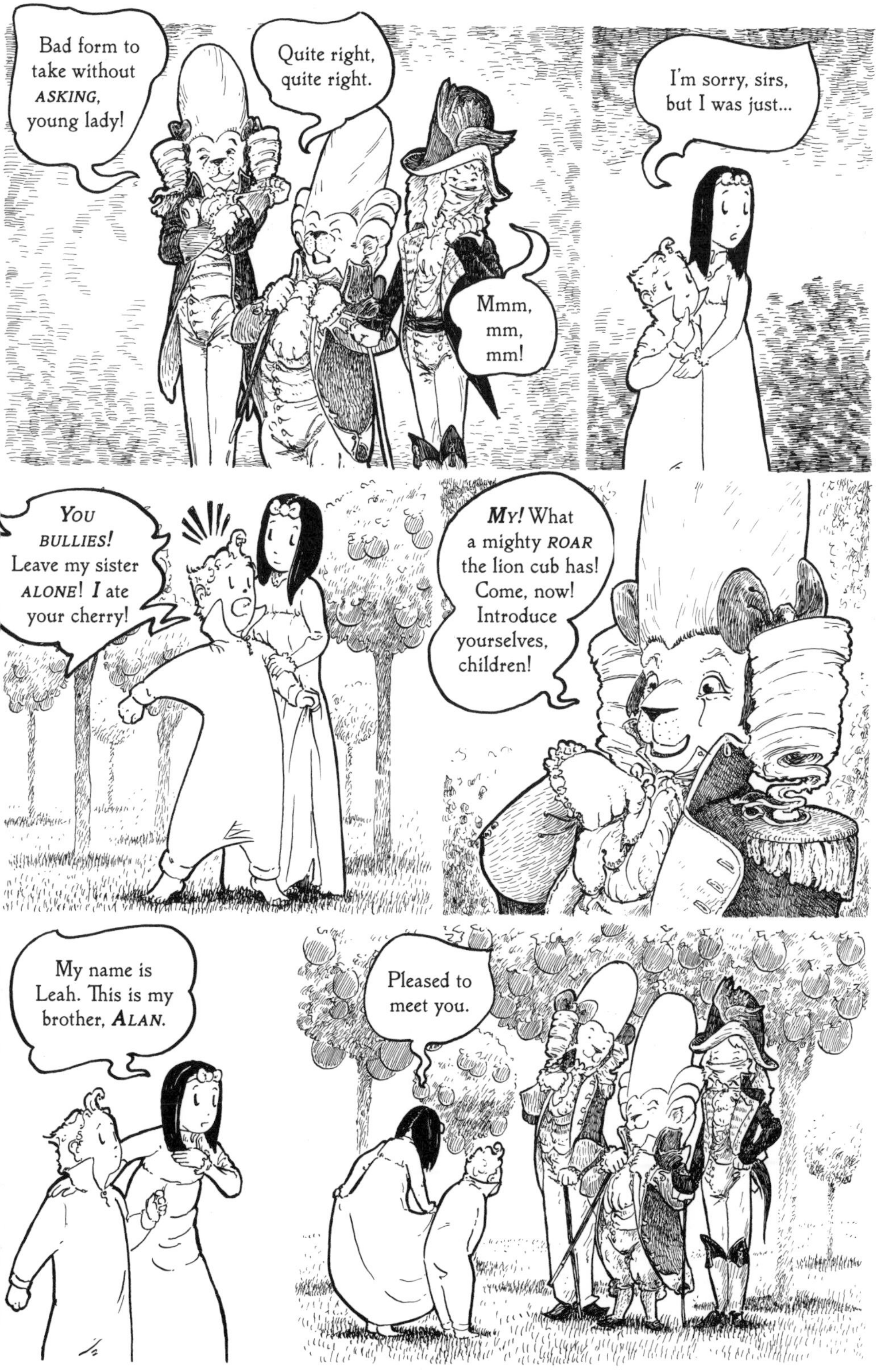
Bad form to take without ASKING, young lady!
Quite right, quite right.
Mmm, mm, mm!
I'm sorry, sirs, but I was just...
YOU BULLIES! Leave my sister ALONE! I ate your cherry!
MY! What a mighty ROAR the lion cub has! Come, now! Introduce yourselves, children!
My name is Leah. This is my brother, ALAN.
Pleased to meet you.

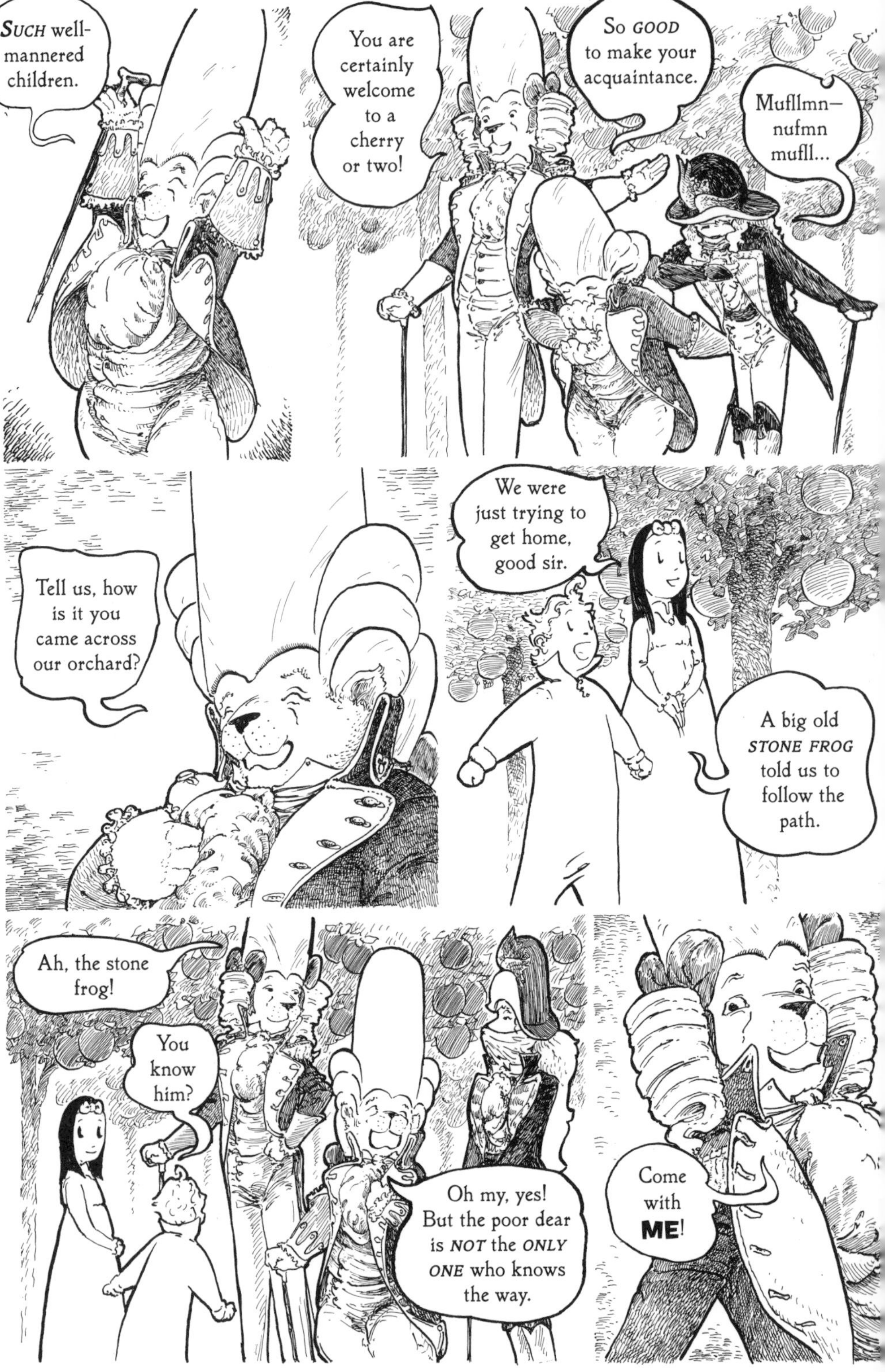

SUCH well-mannered children.
You are certainly welcome to a cherry or two!
So **GOOD** to make your acquaintance.
Mufllmn—nufmn mufll...
Tell us, how is it you came across our orchard?
We were just trying to get home, good sir.
A big old **STONE FROG** told us to follow the path.
Ah, the stone frog!
You know him?
Oh my, yes! But the poor dear is **NOT** the **ONLY ONE** who knows the way.
Come with **ME**!

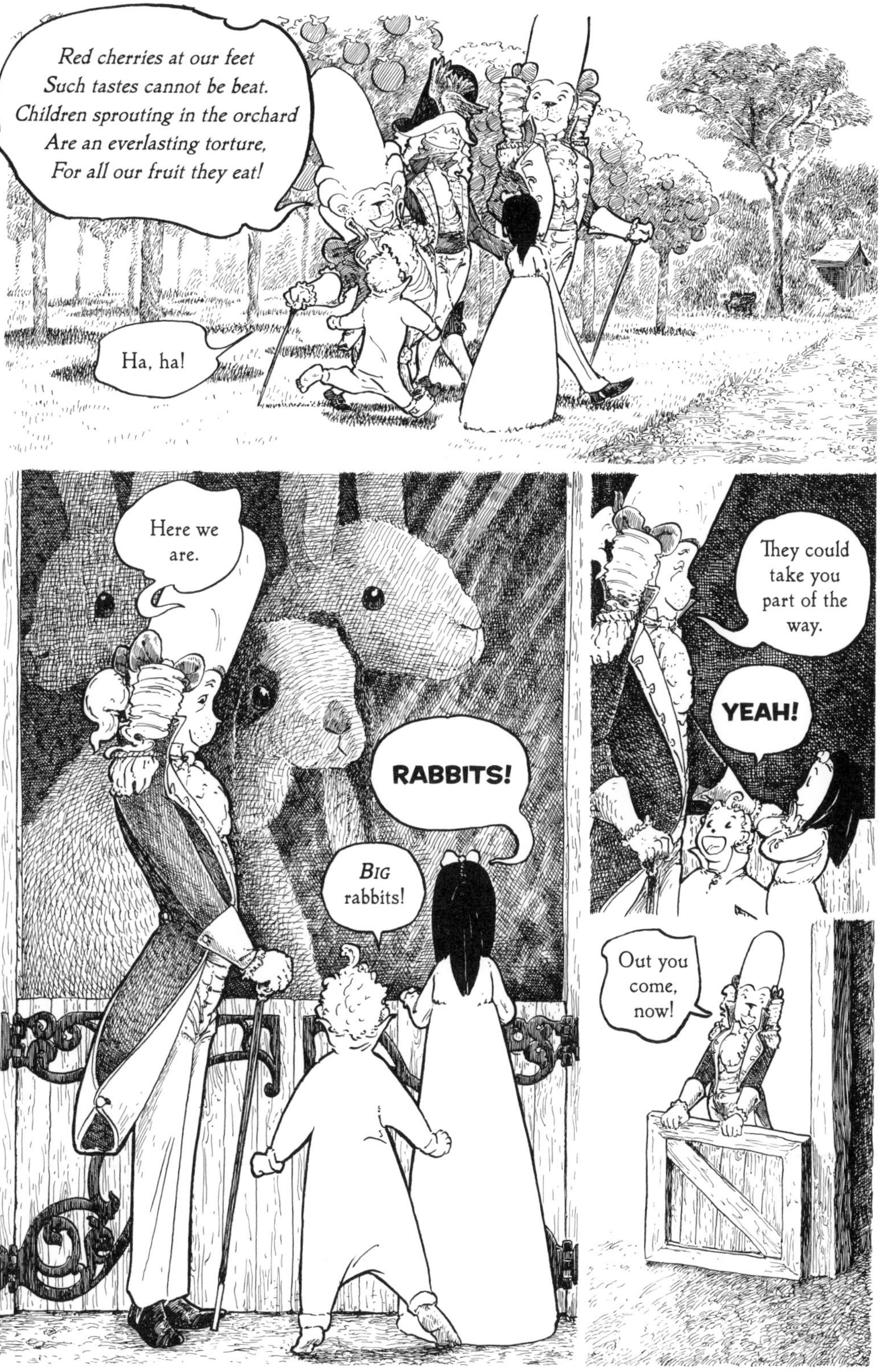
Red cherries at our feet
Such tastes cannot be beat.
Children sprouting in the orchard
Are an everlasting torture,
For all our fruit they eat!
Ha, ha!
Here we are.
RABBITS!
BIG rabbits!
They could take you part of the way.
YEAH!
Out you come, now!

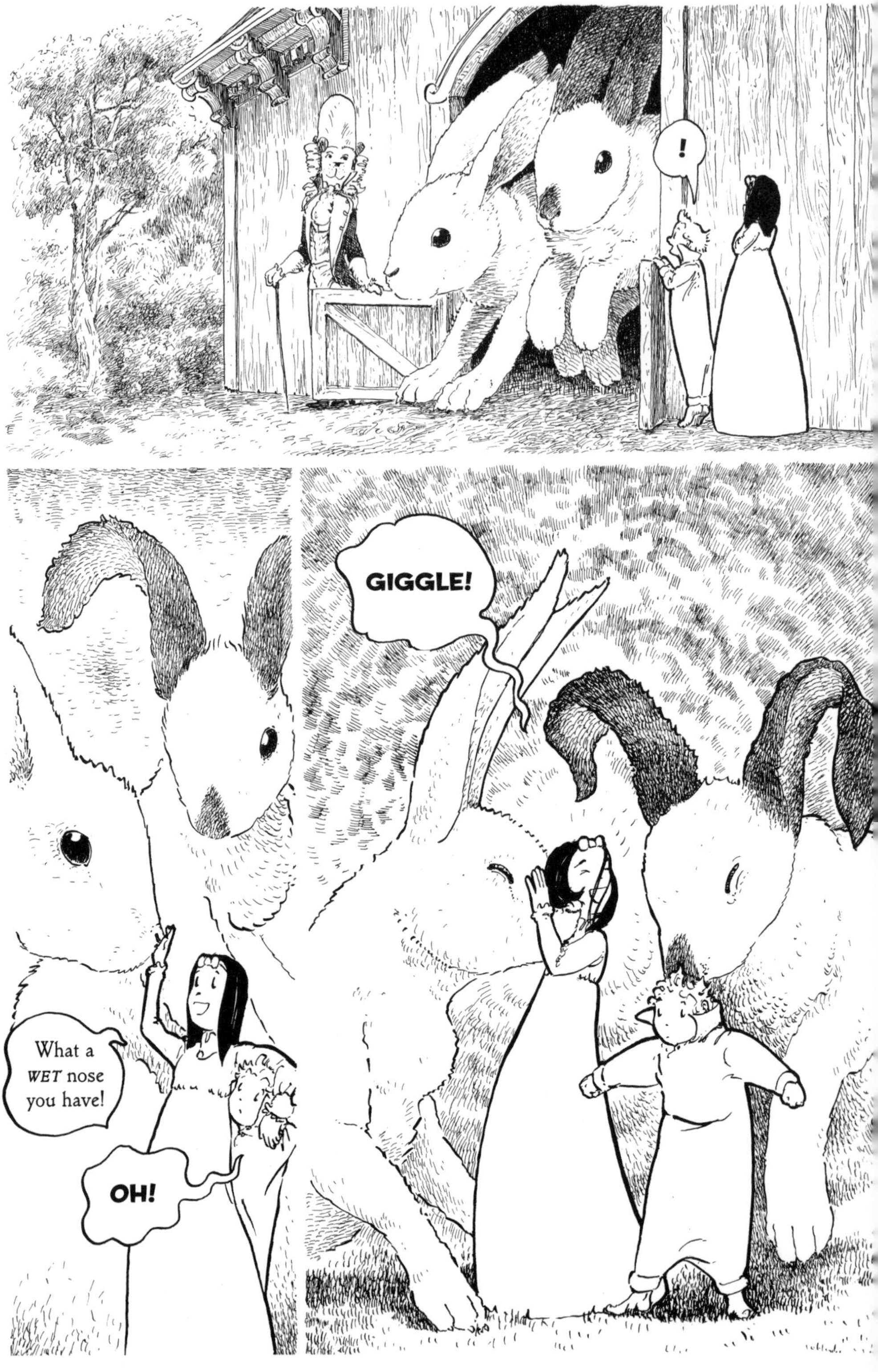
!
What a *WET* nose you have!
OH!
GIGGLE!

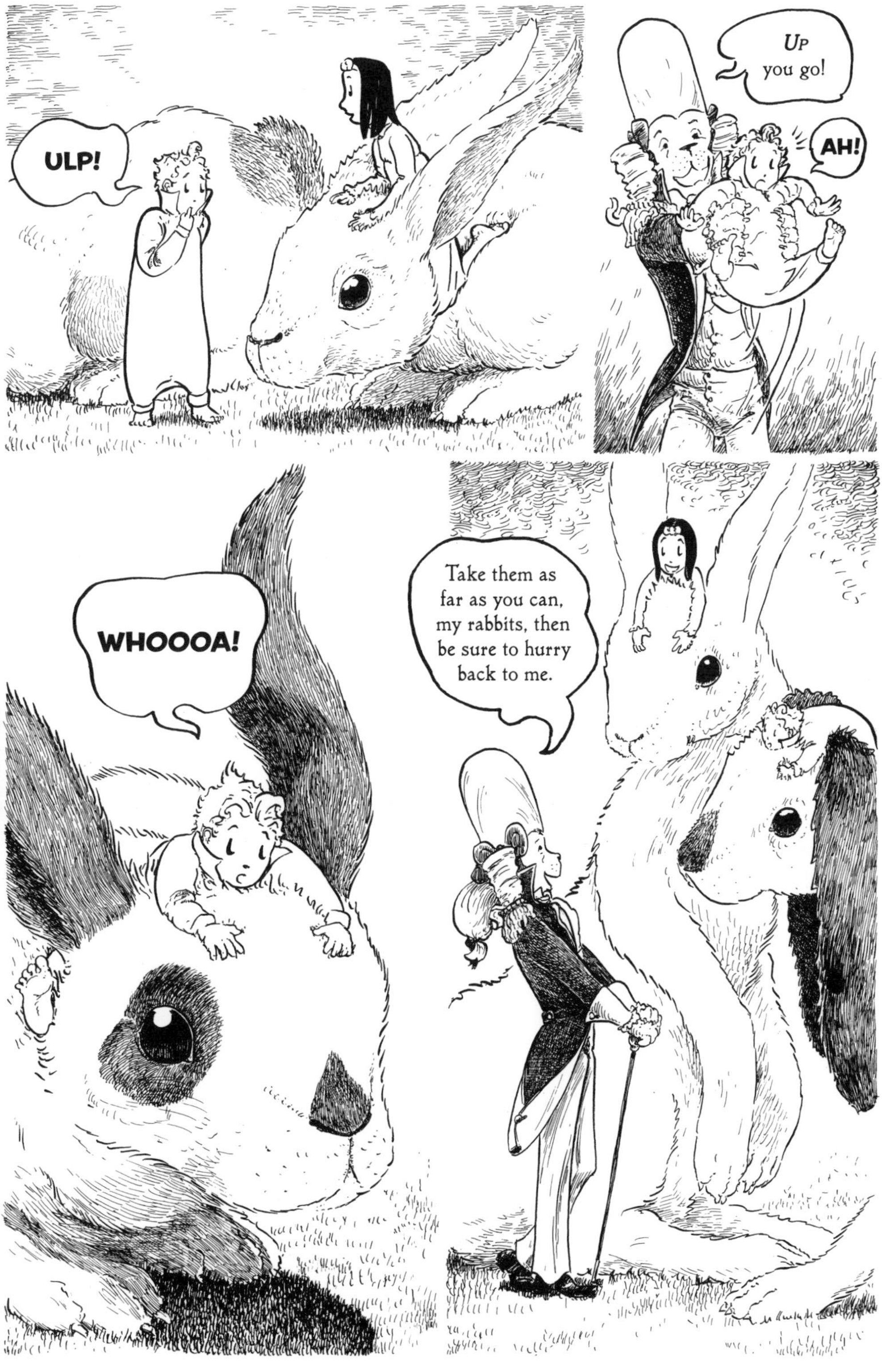
ULP!
UP you go!
AH!
WHOOOA!
Take them as far as you can, my rabbits, then be sure to hurry back to me.

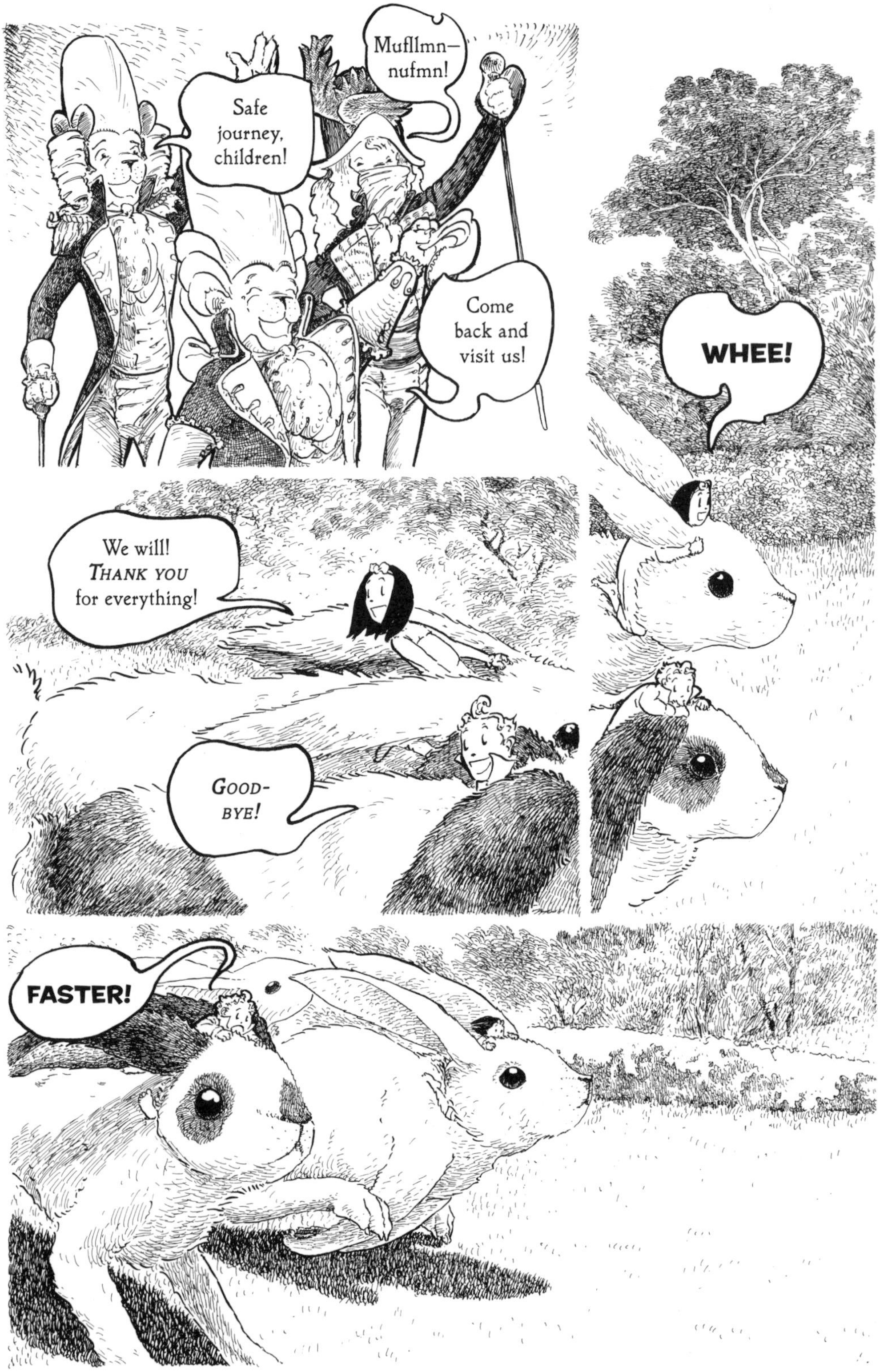
Safe journey, children!
Muflmn— nufmn!
Come back and visit us!
WHEE!
We will! THANK YOU for everything!
GOOD-BYE!
FASTER!

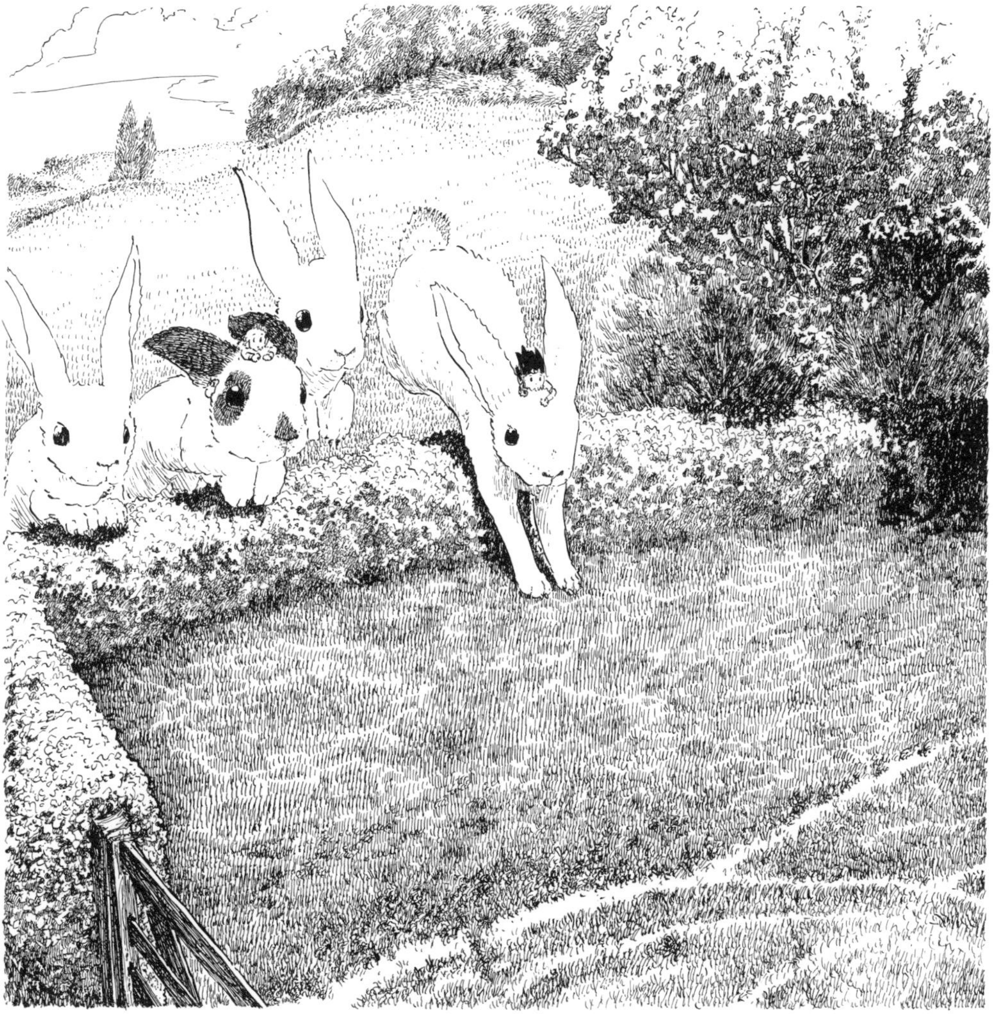

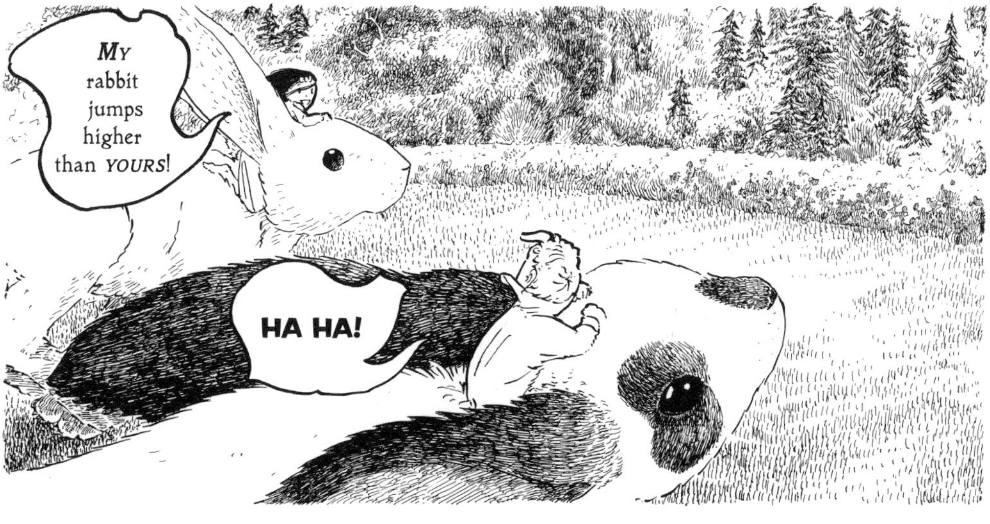
MY rabbit jumps higher than YOURS!
HA HA!

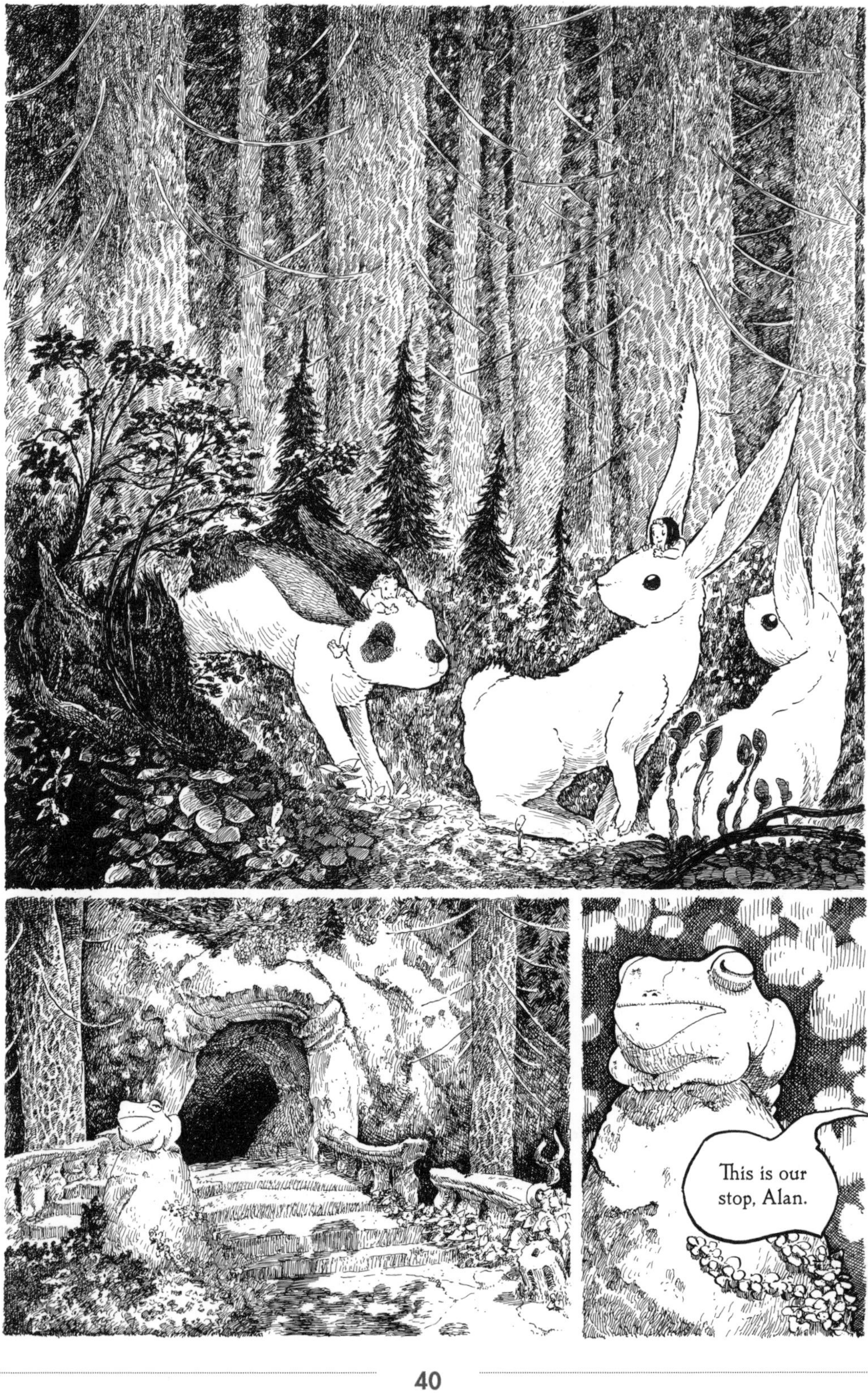
This is our stop, Alan.

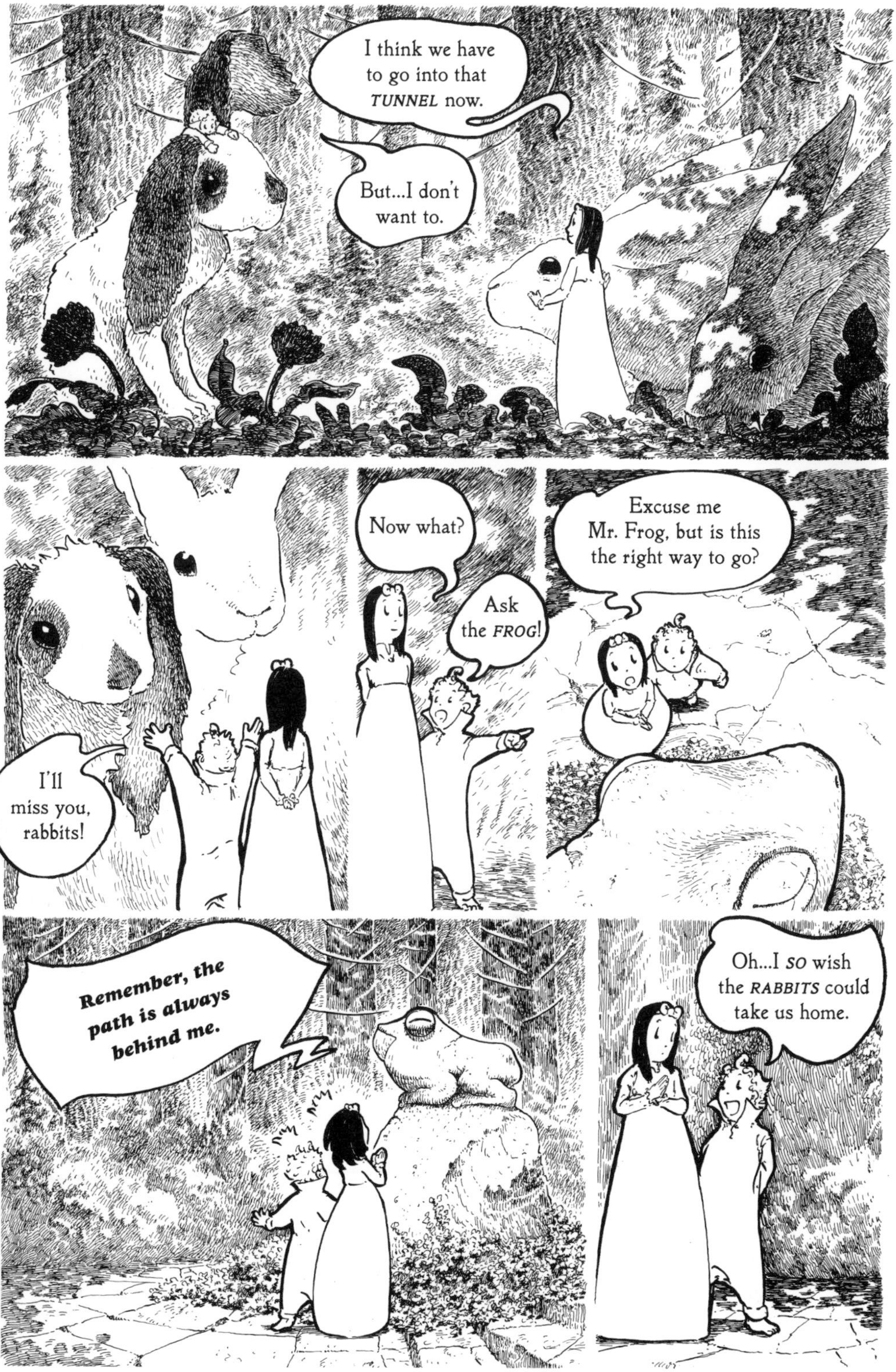
I think we have to go into that TUNNEL now.
But...I don't want to.
I'll miss you, rabbits!
Now what?
Ask the FROG!
Excuse me Mr. Frog, but is this the right way to go?
Remember, the path is always behind me.
Oh...I SO wish the RABBITS could take us home.

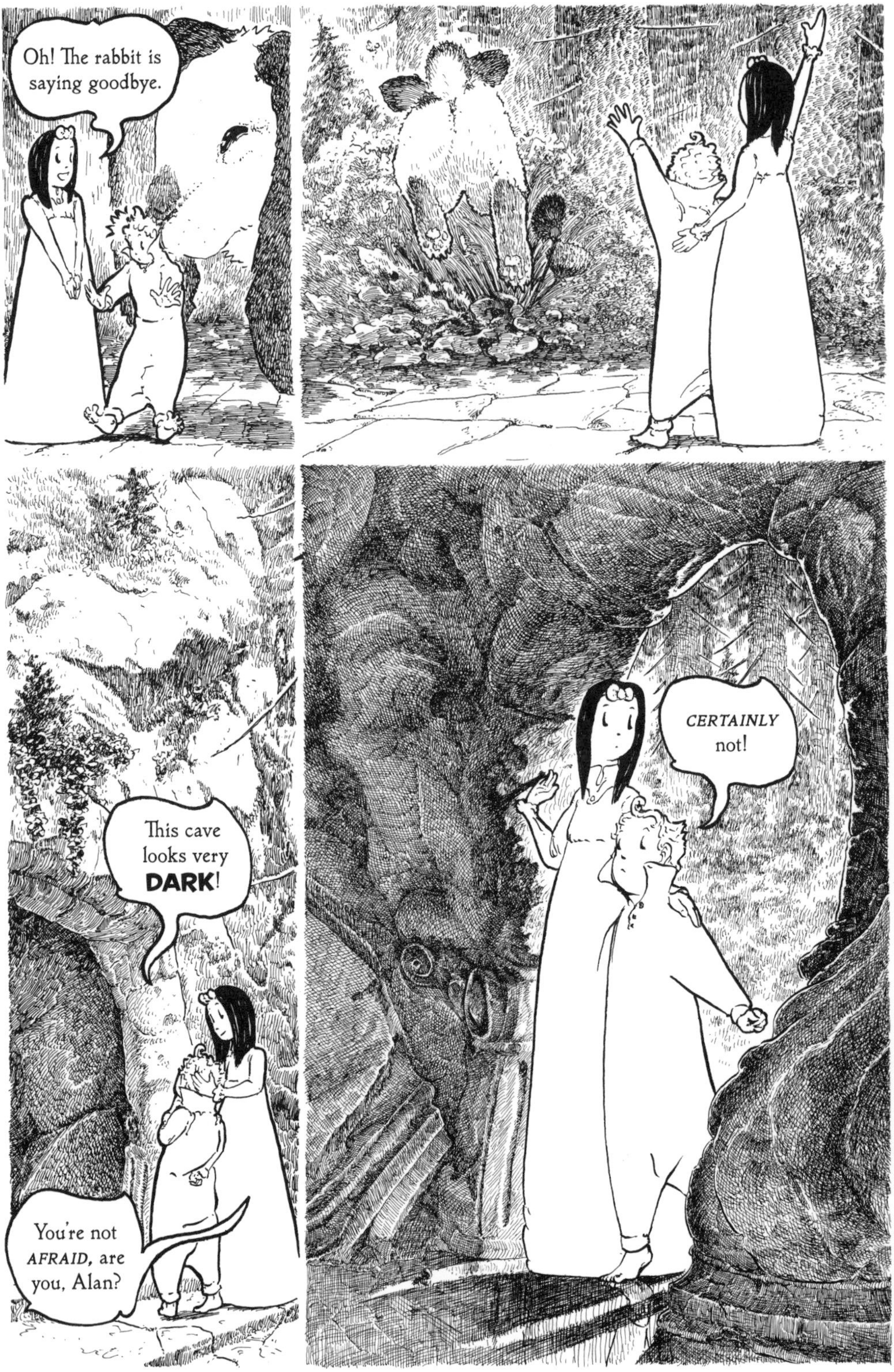

Oh! The rabbit is saying goodbye.
This cave looks very **DARK**!
You're not *AFRAID*, are you, Alan?
CERTAINLY not!

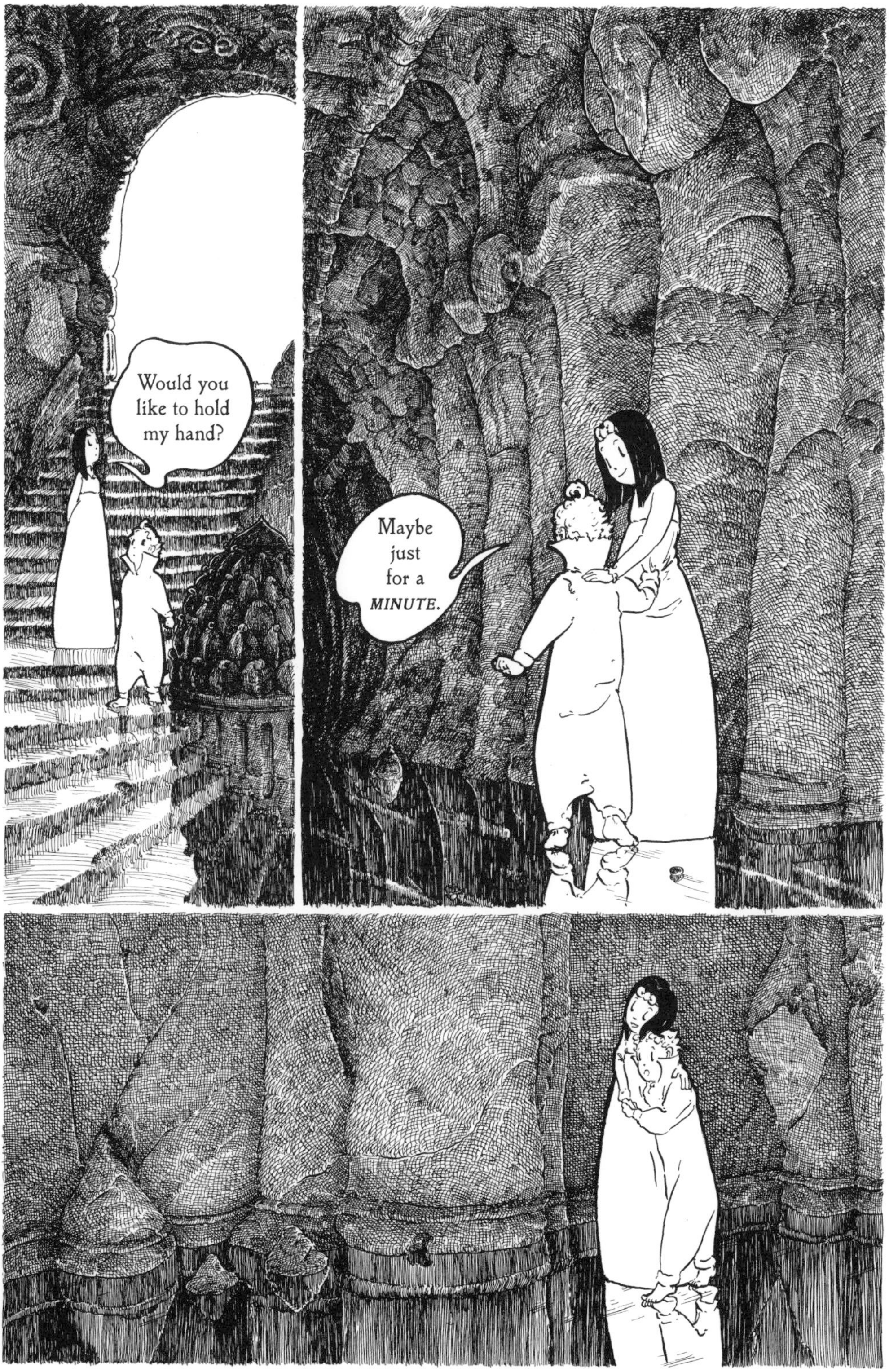
Would you like to hold my hand?
Maybe just for a *MINUTE.*

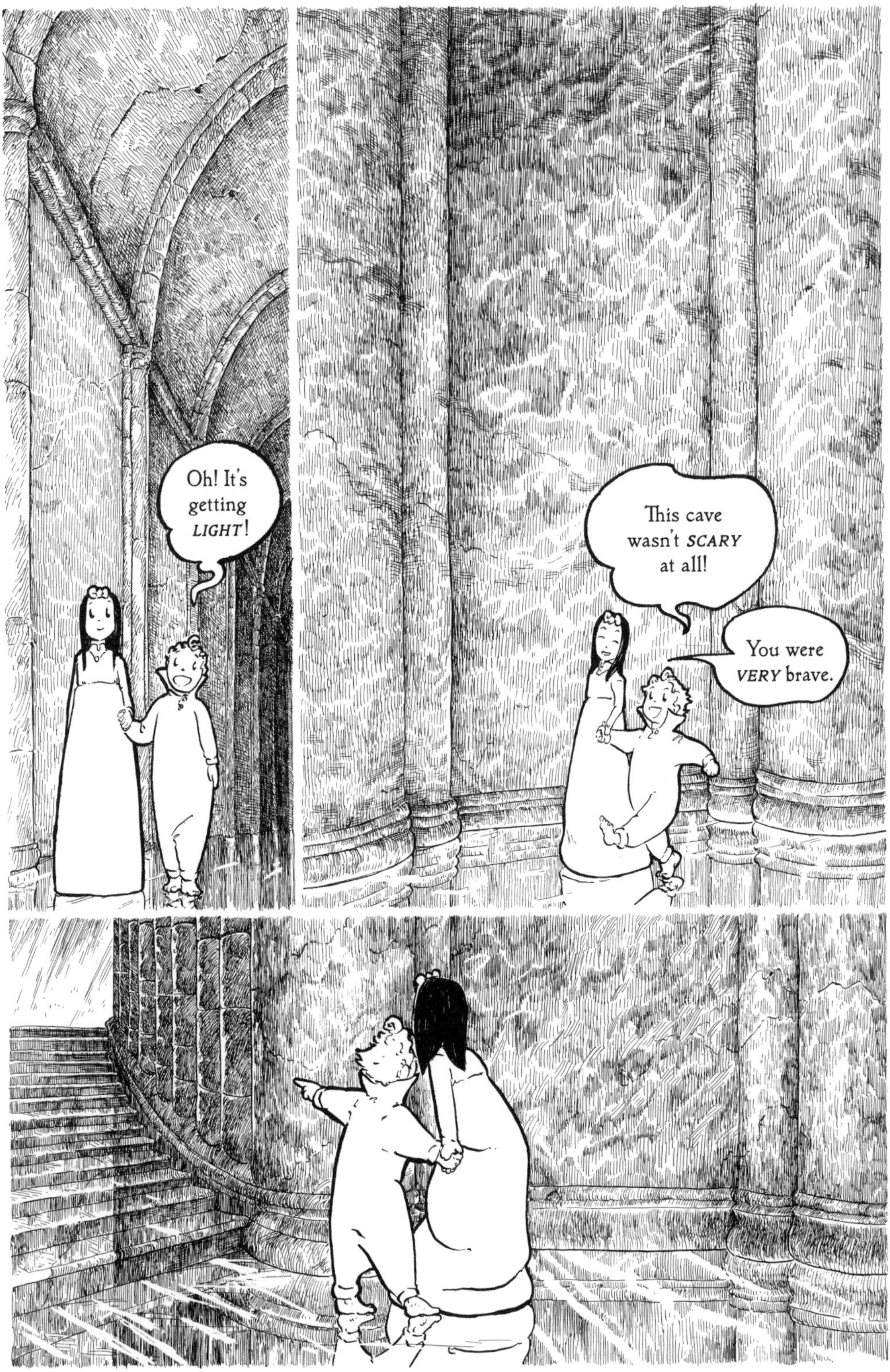
Oh! It's getting *LIGHT*!
This cave wasn't *SCARY* at all!
You were *VERY* brave.

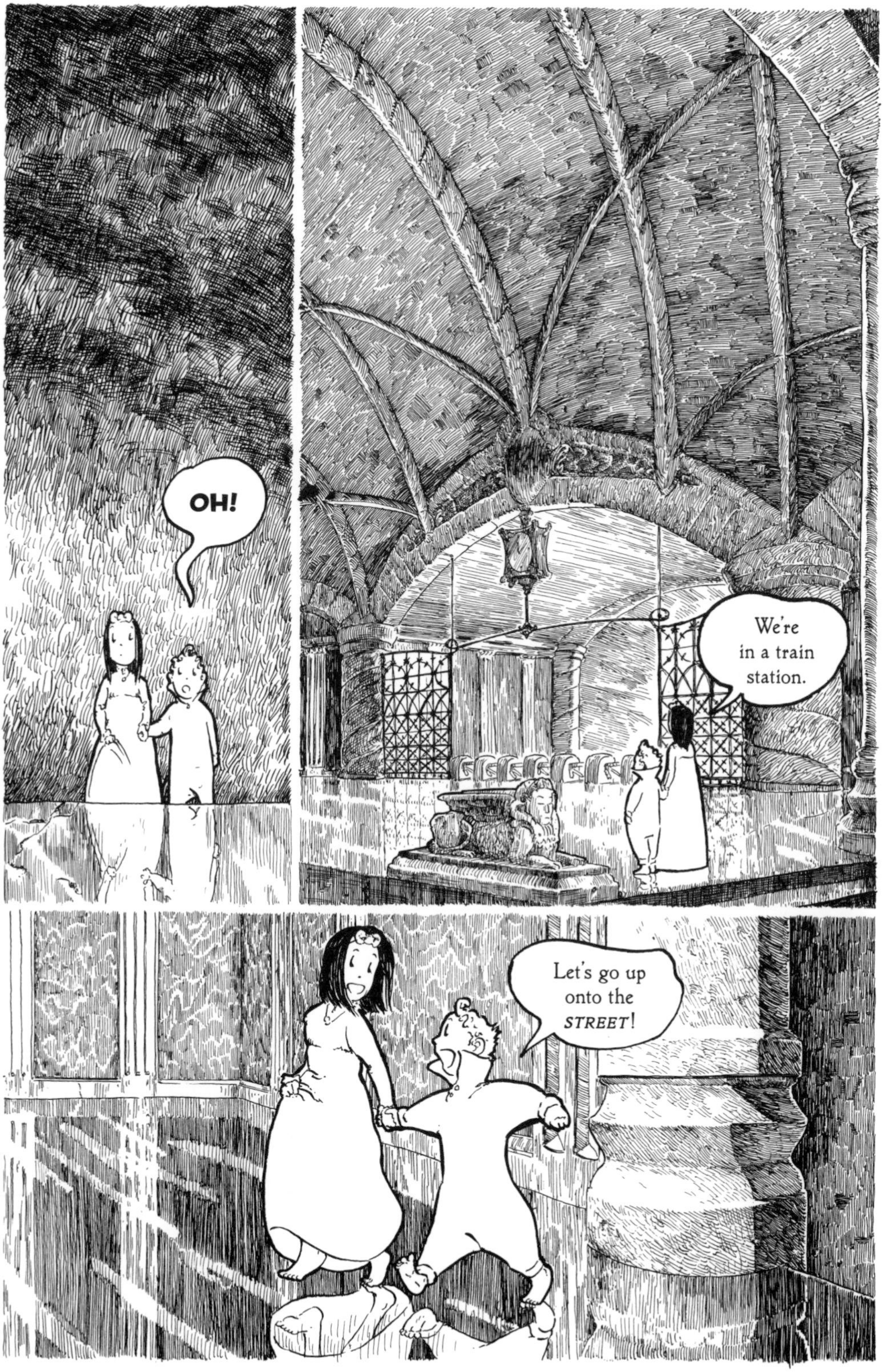
OH!
We're in a train station.
Let's go up onto the *STREET*!

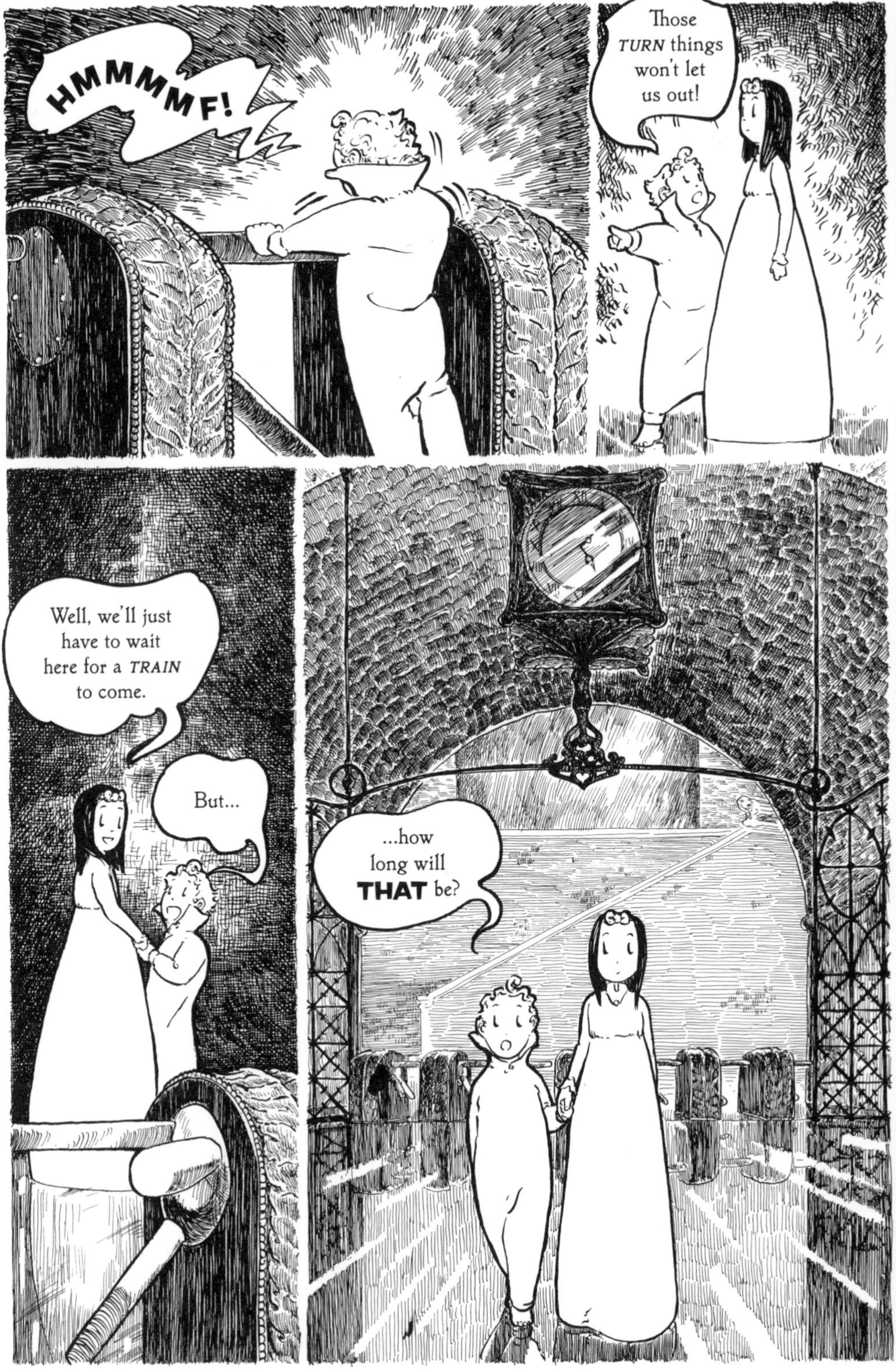
HMMMMF!
Those TURN things won't let us out!
Well, we'll just have to wait here for a TRAIN to come.
But...
...how long will THAT be?

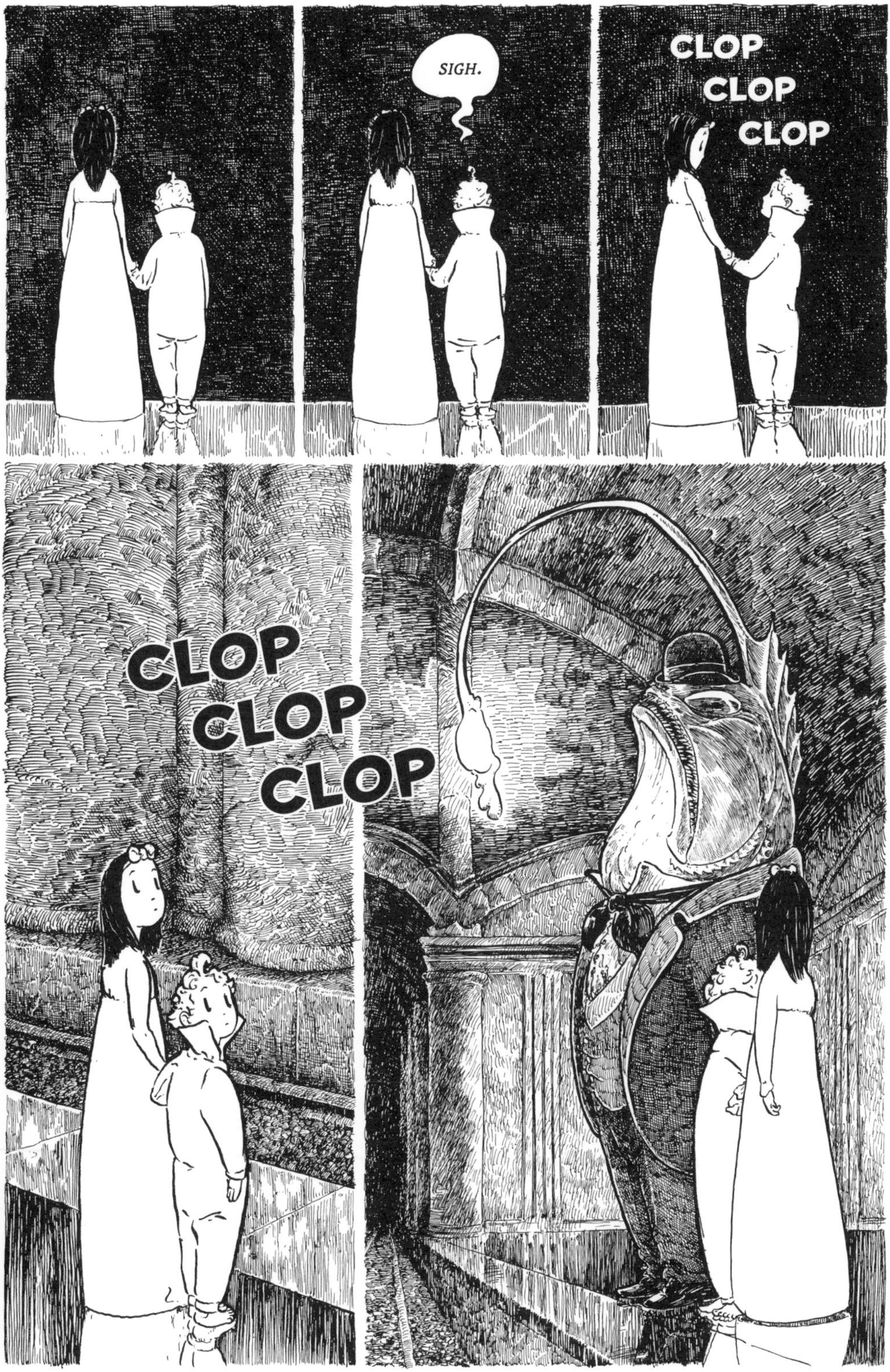
SIGH.
CLOP
CLOP
CLOP
CLOP
CLOP
CLOP

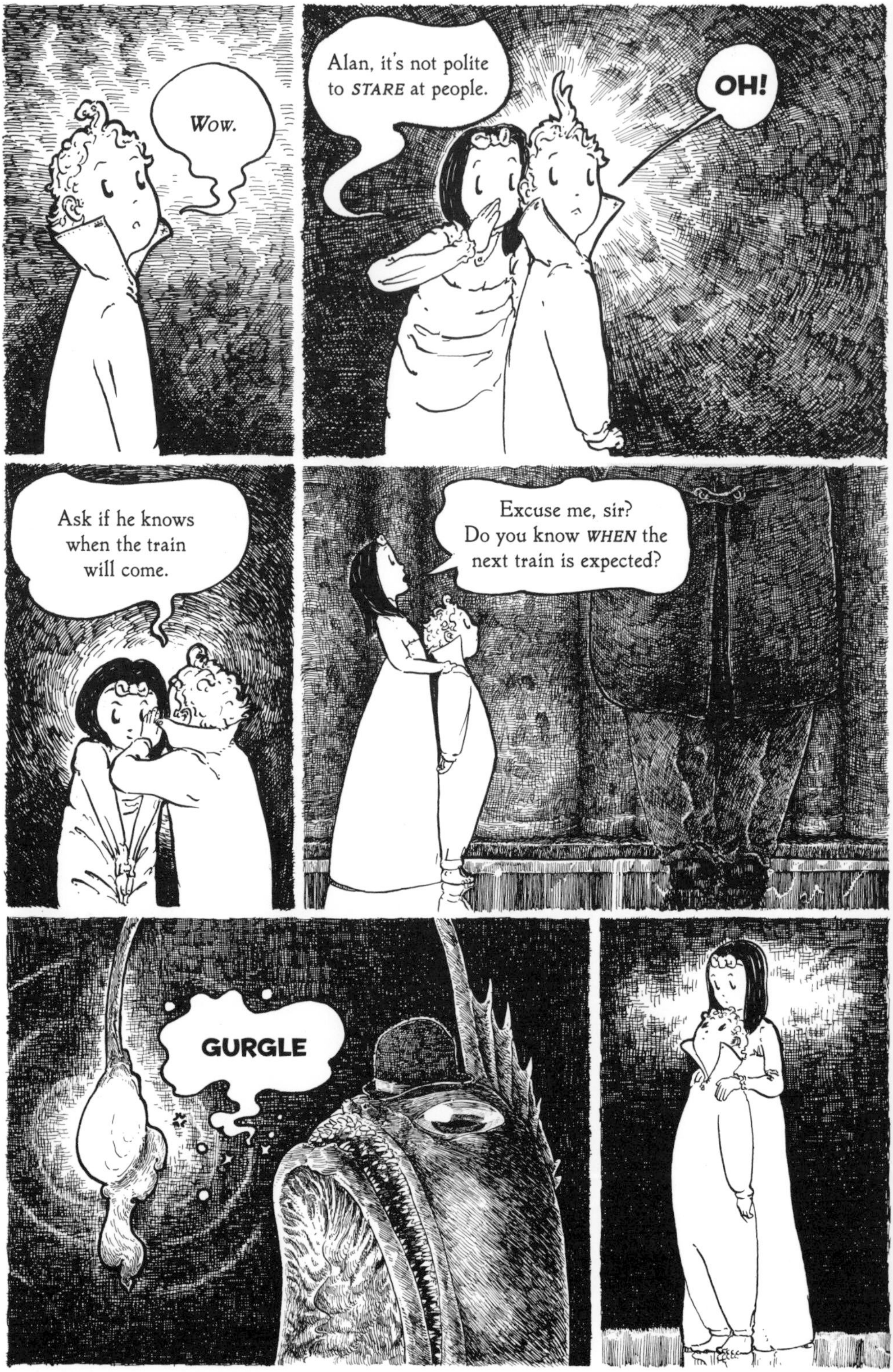

Wow.
Alan, it's not polite to STARE at people.
OH!
Ask if he knows when the train will come.
Excuse me, sir? Do you know WHEN the next train is expected?
GURGLE

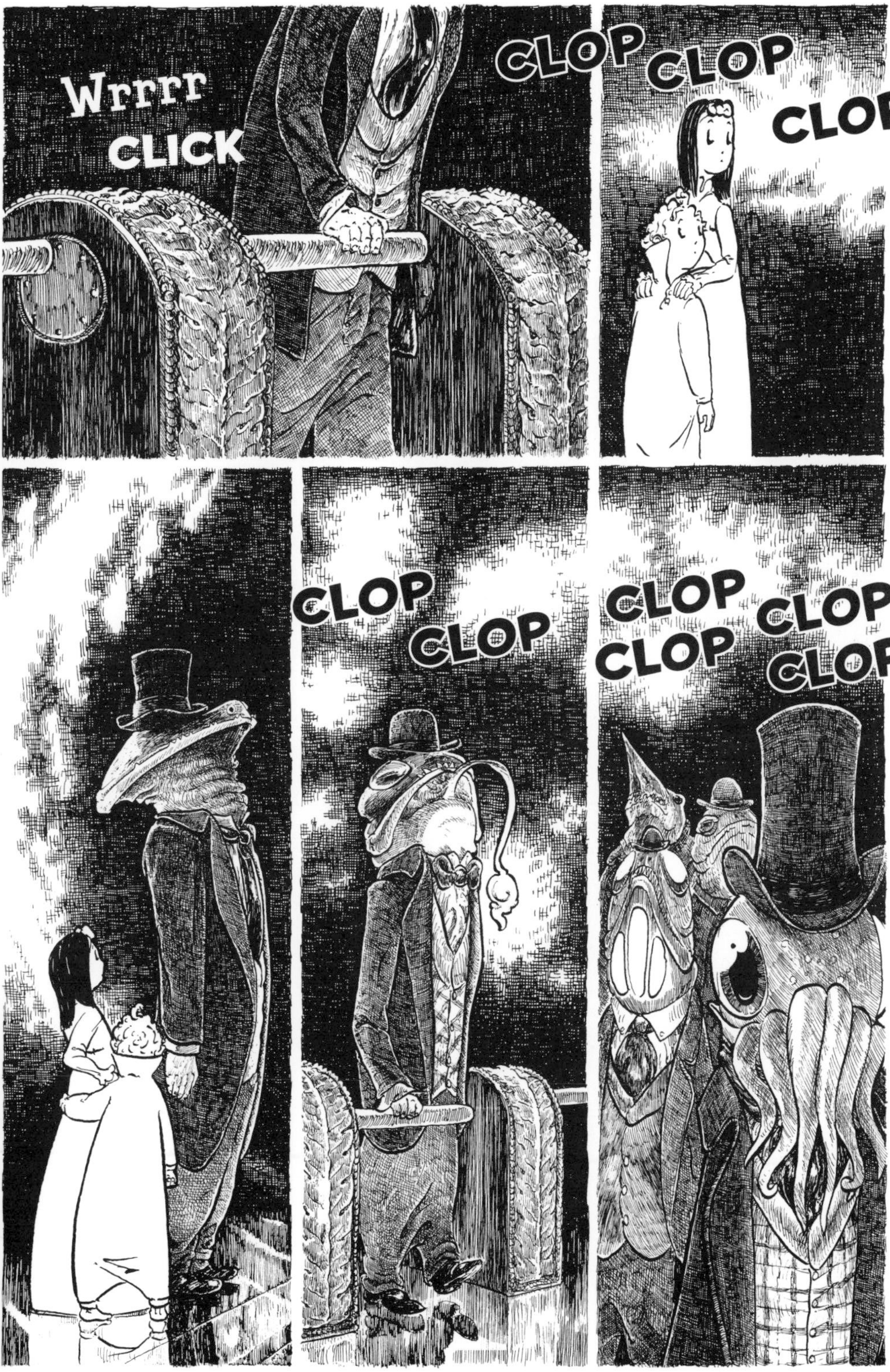
Wrrrr
CLICK
CLOP
CLOP
CLOP
CLOP
CLOP
CLOP
CLOP
CLOP
CLOP

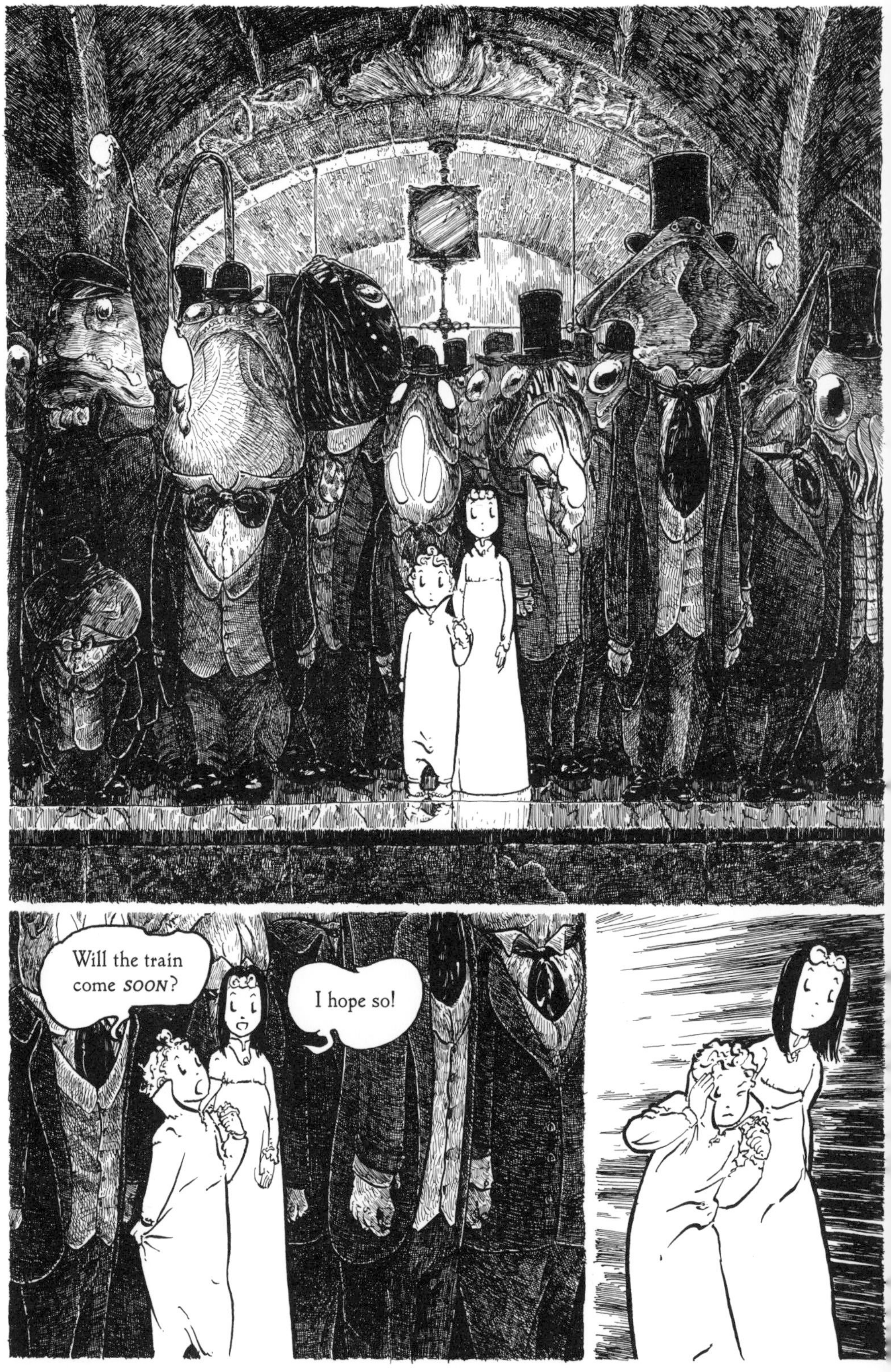
Will the train come *SOON*?
I hope so!

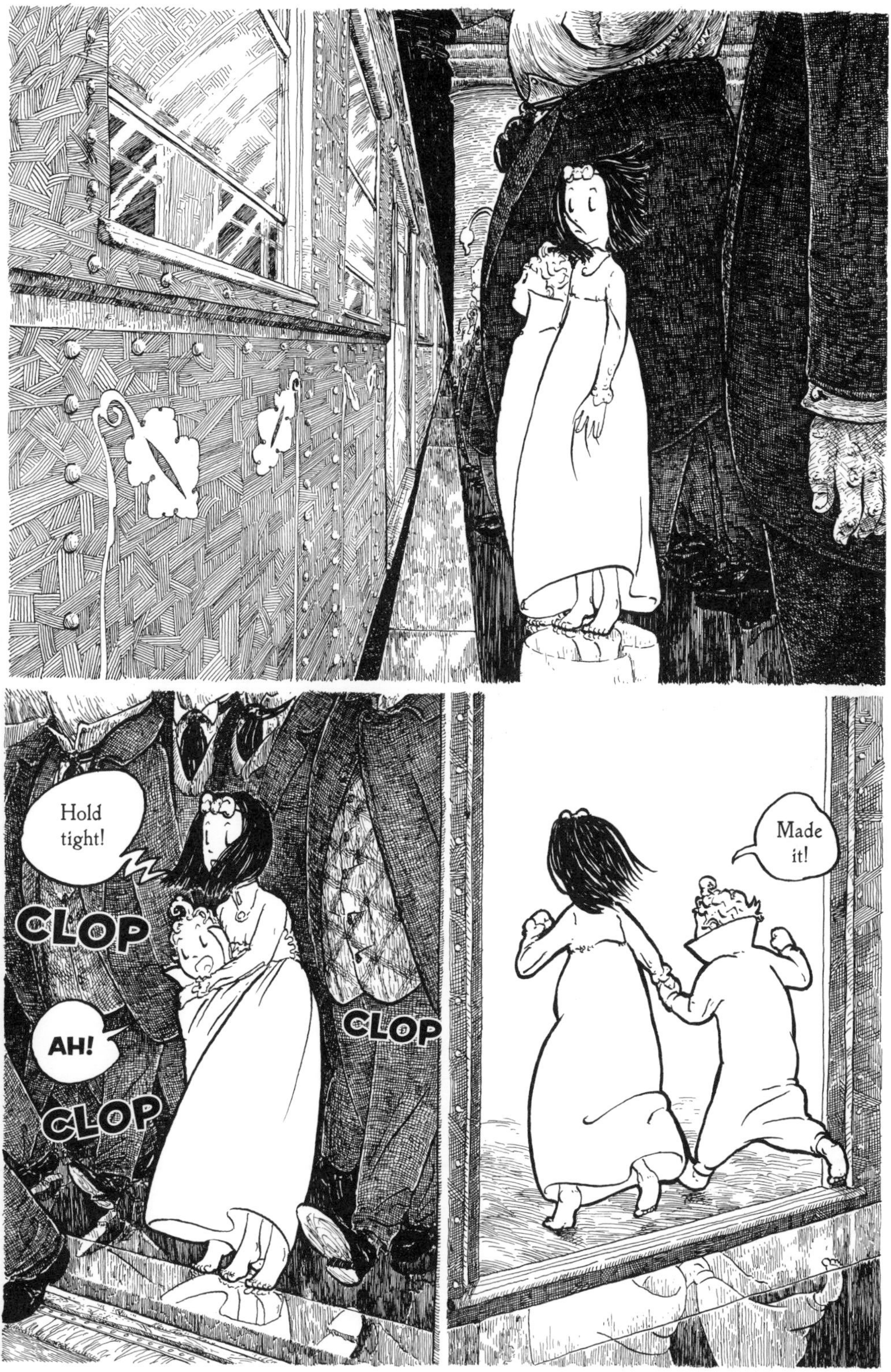
Hold tight!
CLOP
AH!
CLOP
CLOP
Made it!

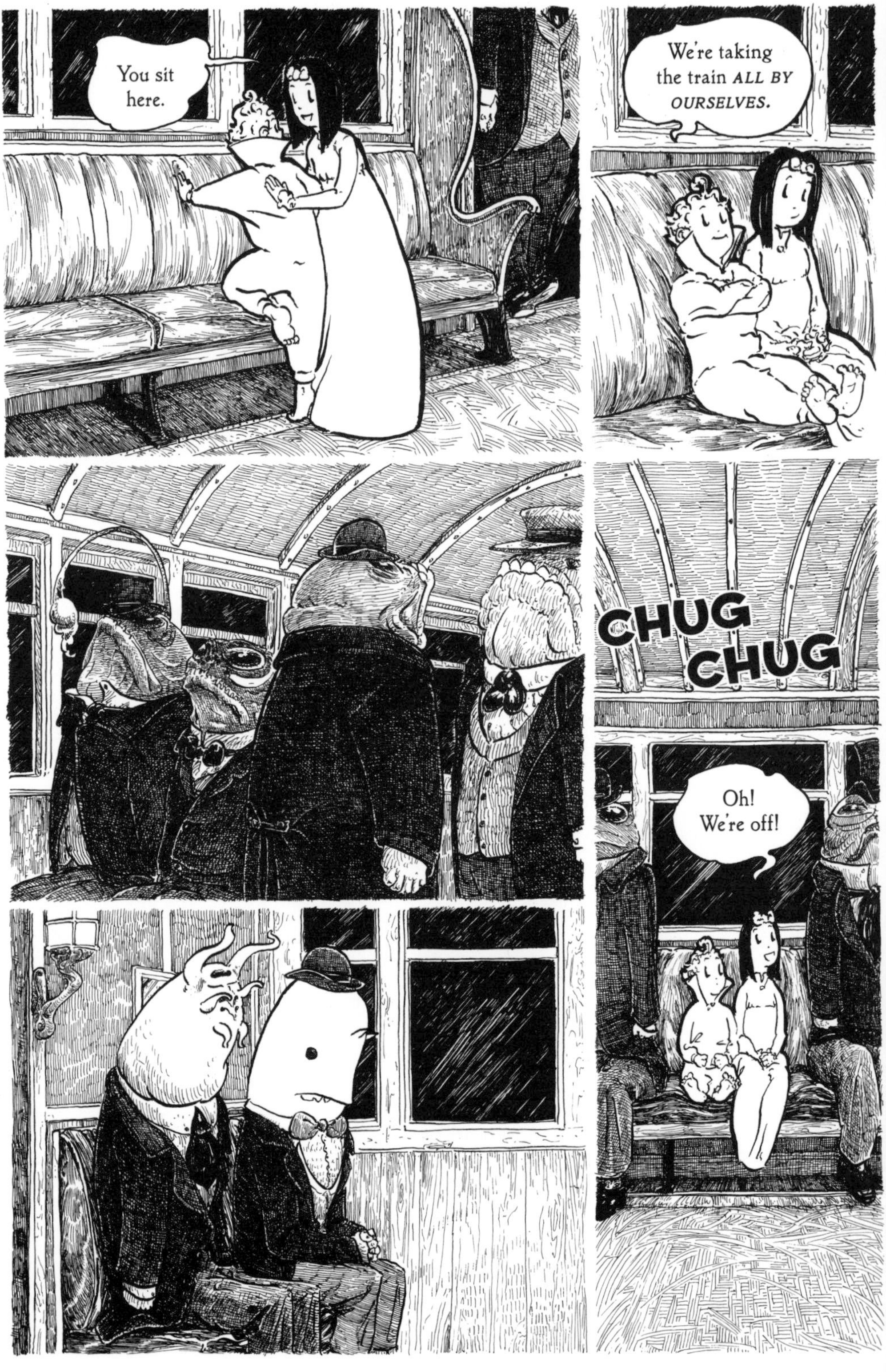
You sit here.
We're taking the train *ALL BY OURSELVES.*
CHUG CHUG
Oh! We're off!

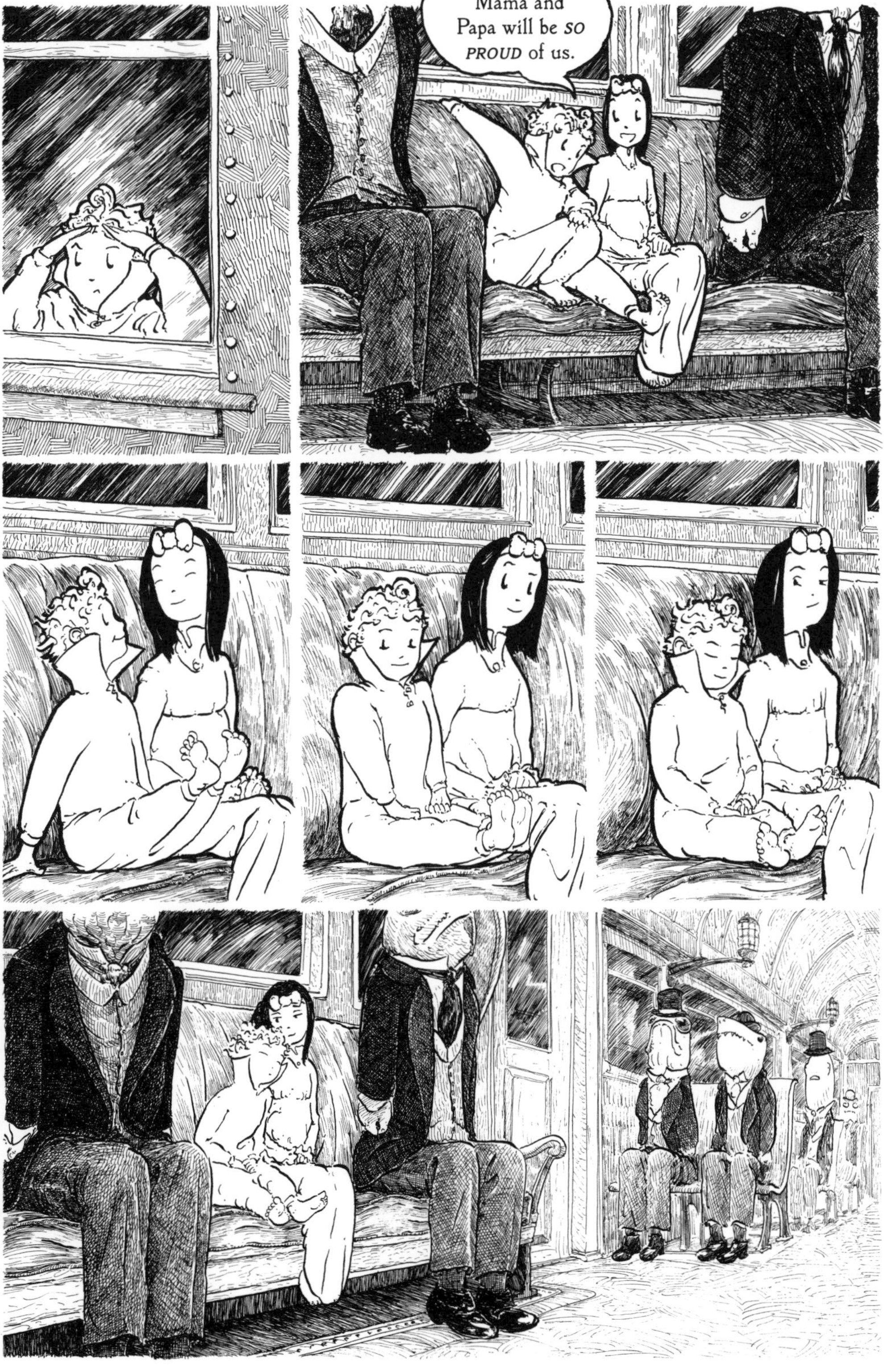
Mama and Papa will be SO PROUD of us.

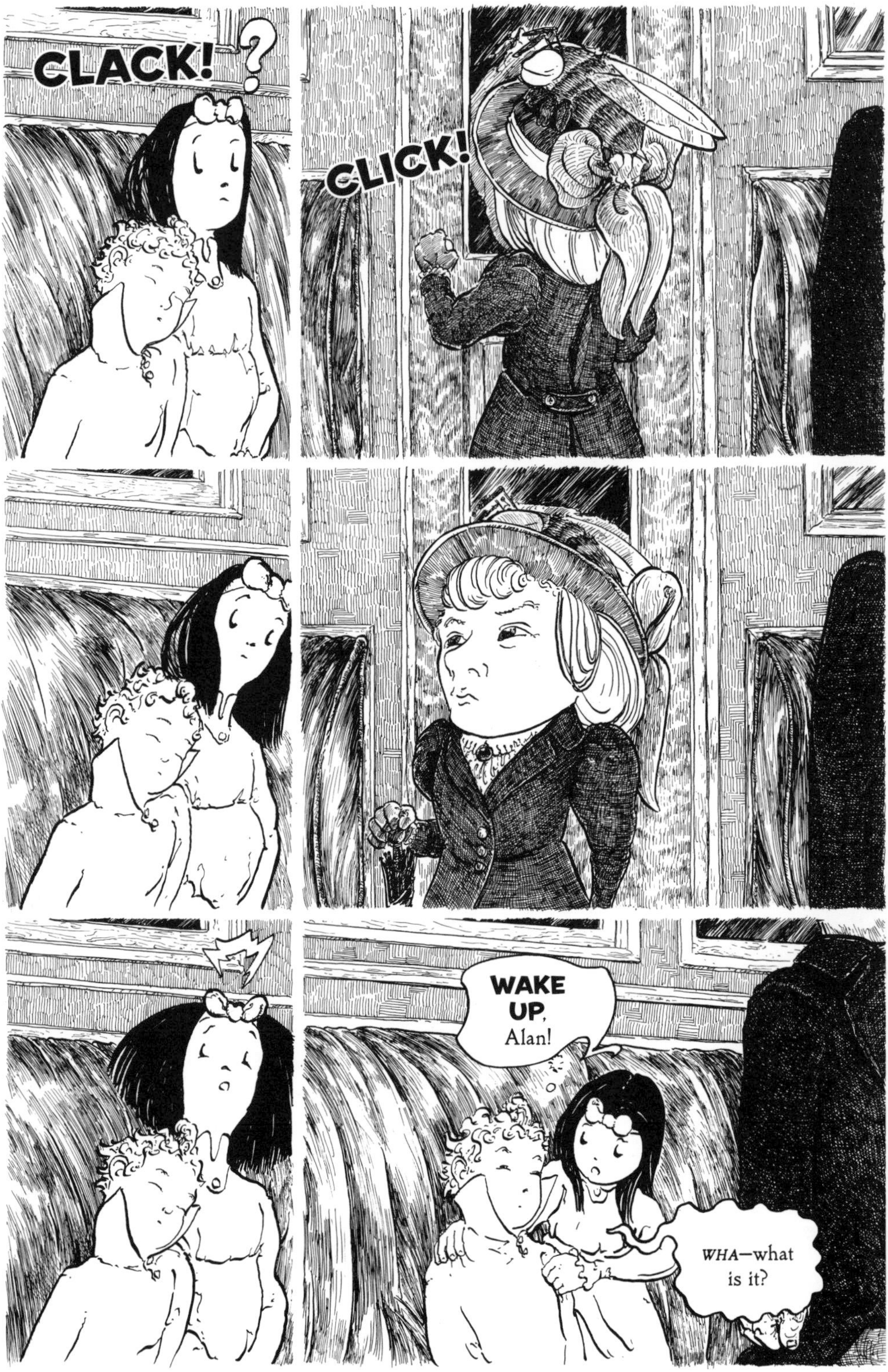
CLACK!
?
CLICK!
WAKE UP, Alan!
WHA—what is it?

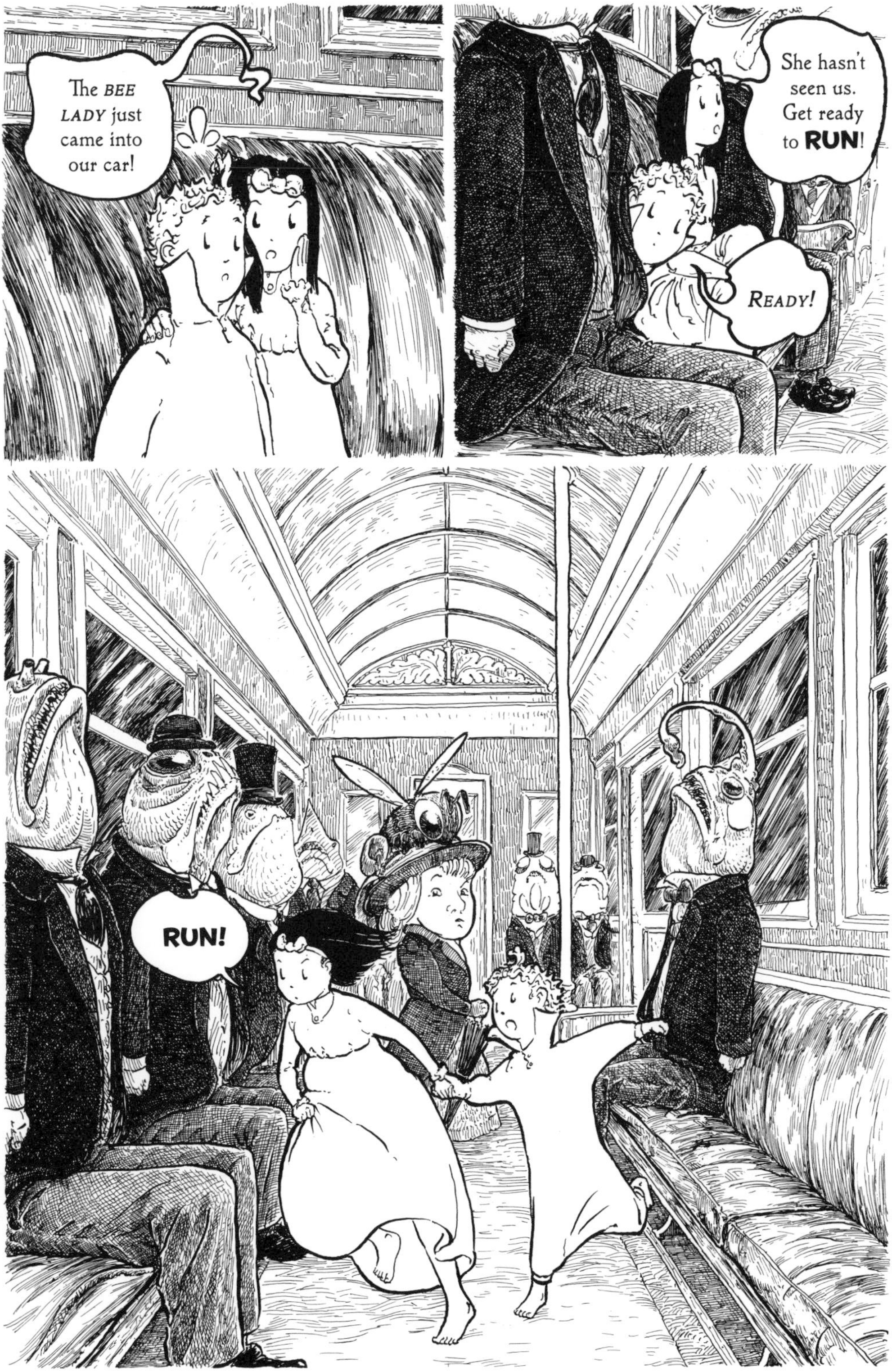
The *BEE LADY* just came into our car!
She hasn't seen us. Get ready to **RUN**!
READY!
RUN!

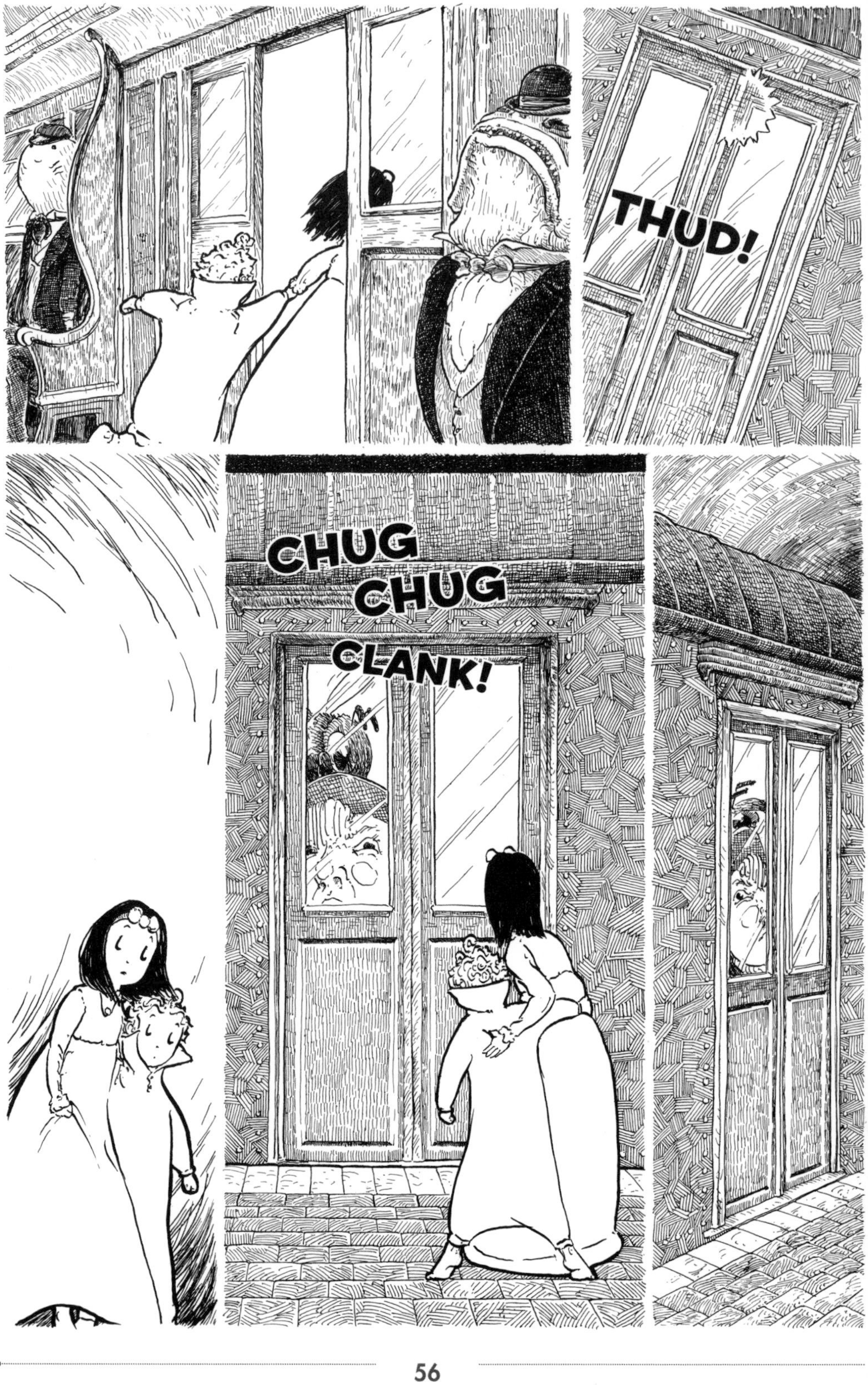
THUD!
CHUG
CHUG
CLANK!

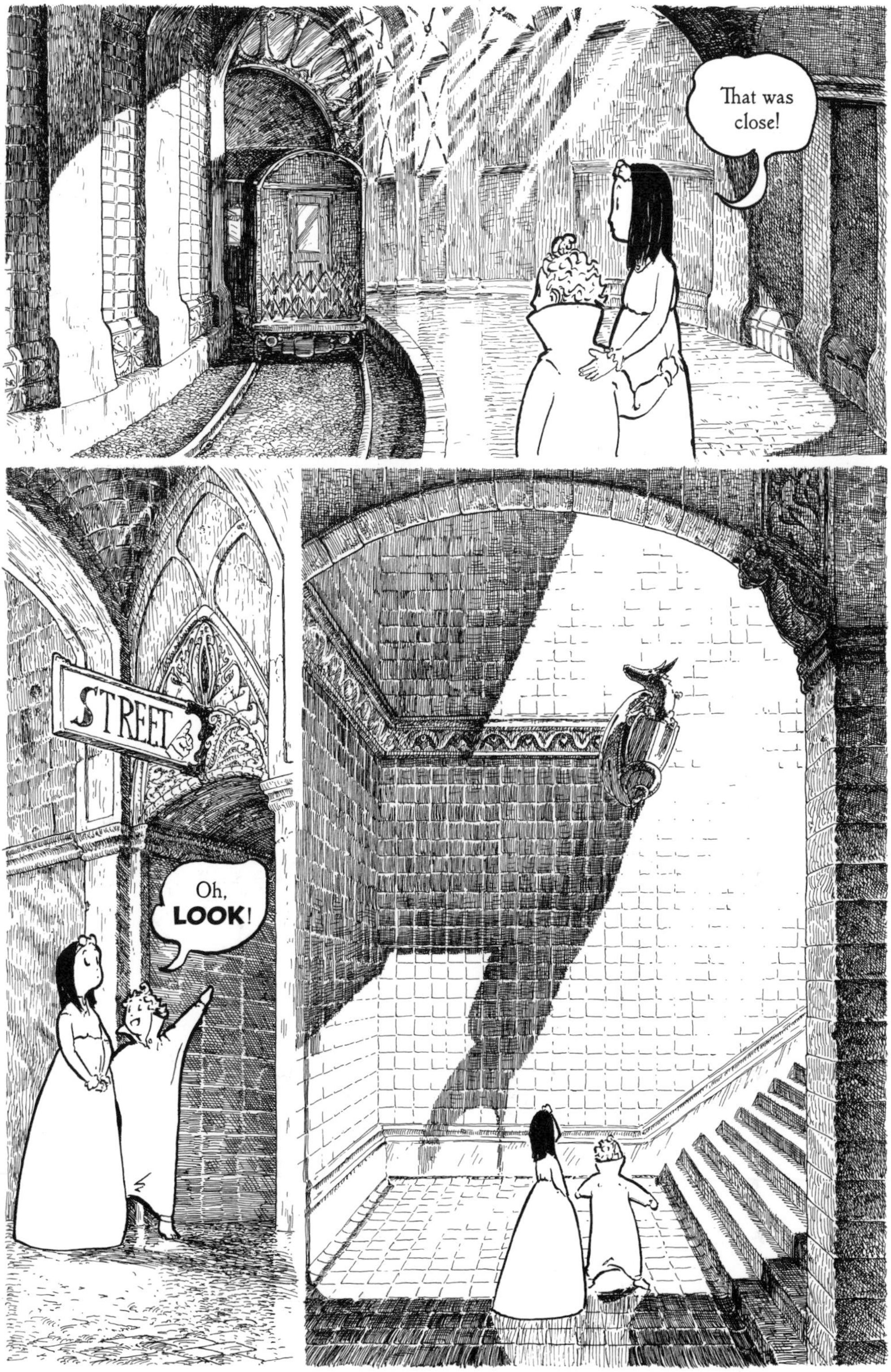
That was close!
STREET
Oh, **LOOK**!

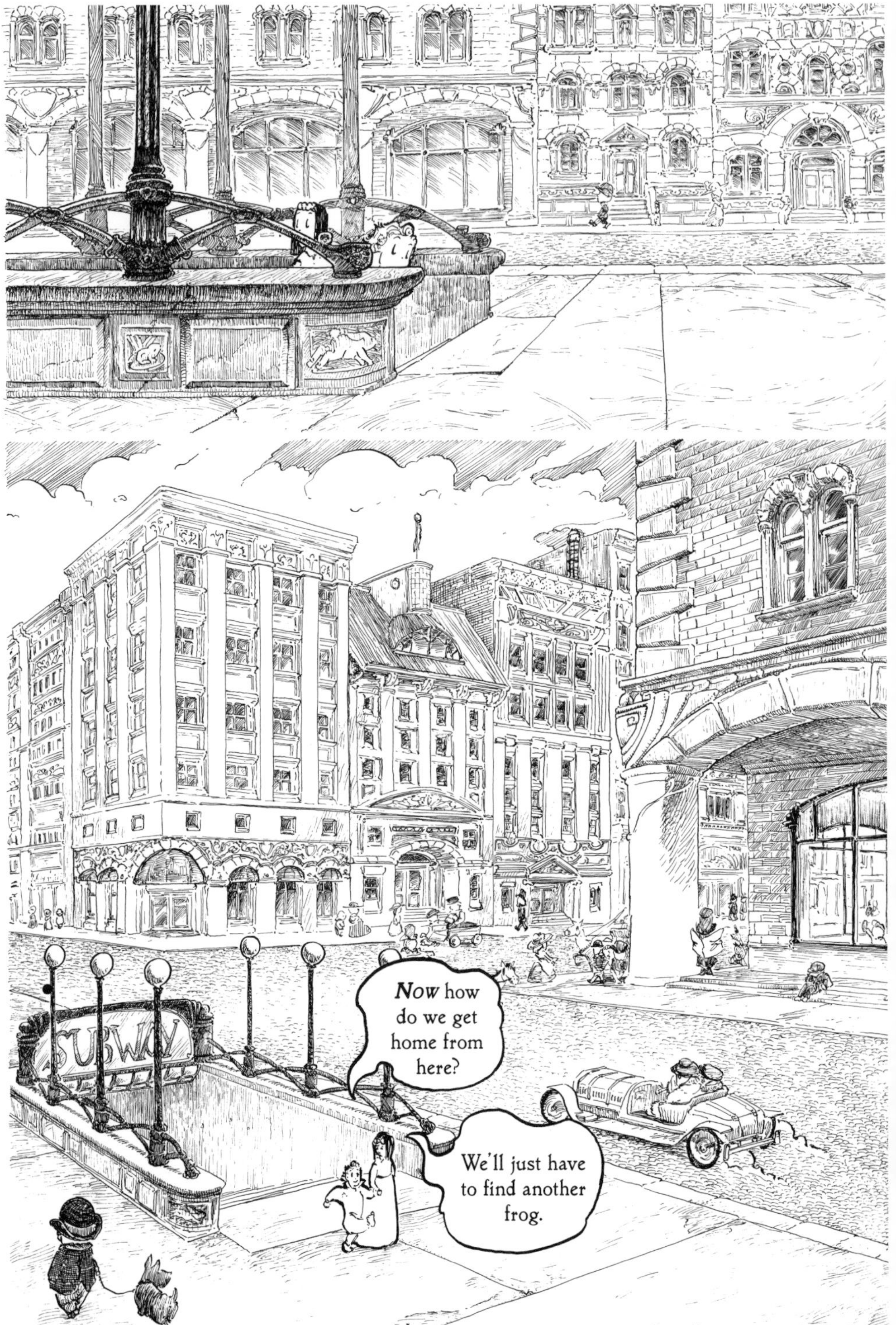
SUBWAY
Now how do we get home from here?
We'll just have to find another frog.

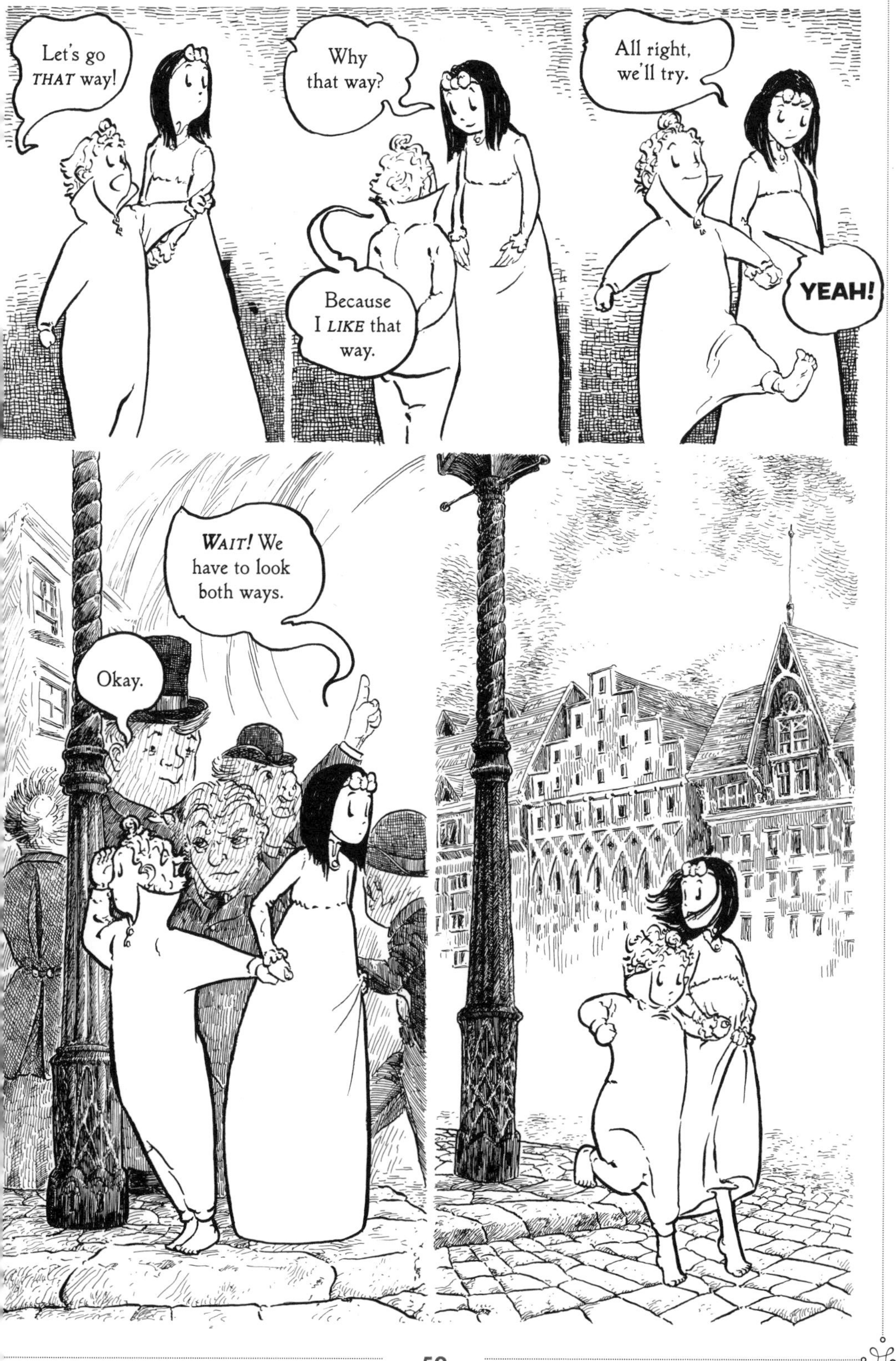
Let's go THAT way!
Why that way?
Because I LIKE that way.
All right, we'll try.
YEAH!
WAIT! We have to look both ways.
Okay.

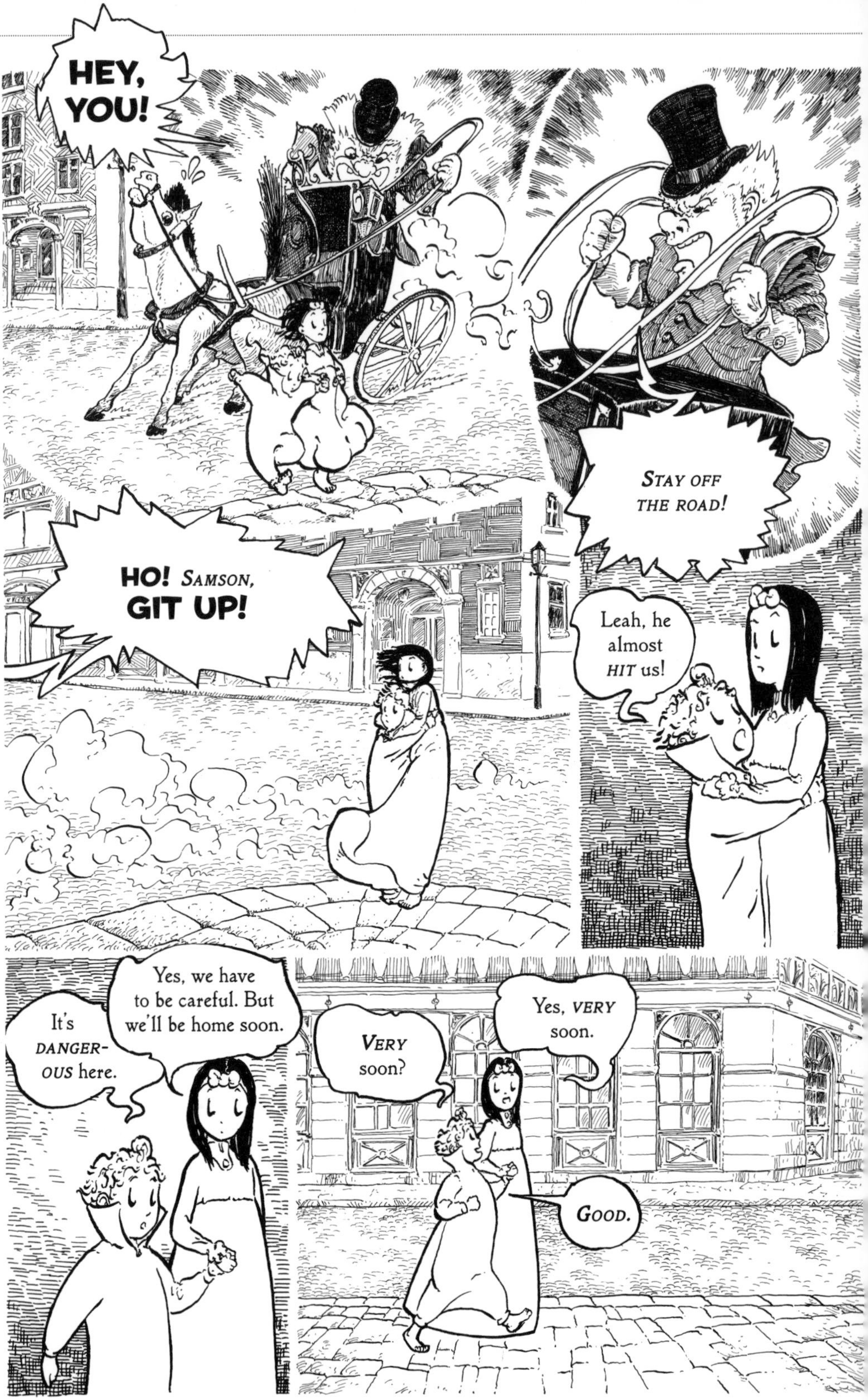
HEY, YOU!
STAY OFF THE ROAD!
HO! SAMSON, GIT UP!
Leah, he almost HIT us!
It's DANGER-OUS here.
Yes, we have to be careful. But we'll be home soon.
VERY soon?
Yes, VERY soon.
GOOD.

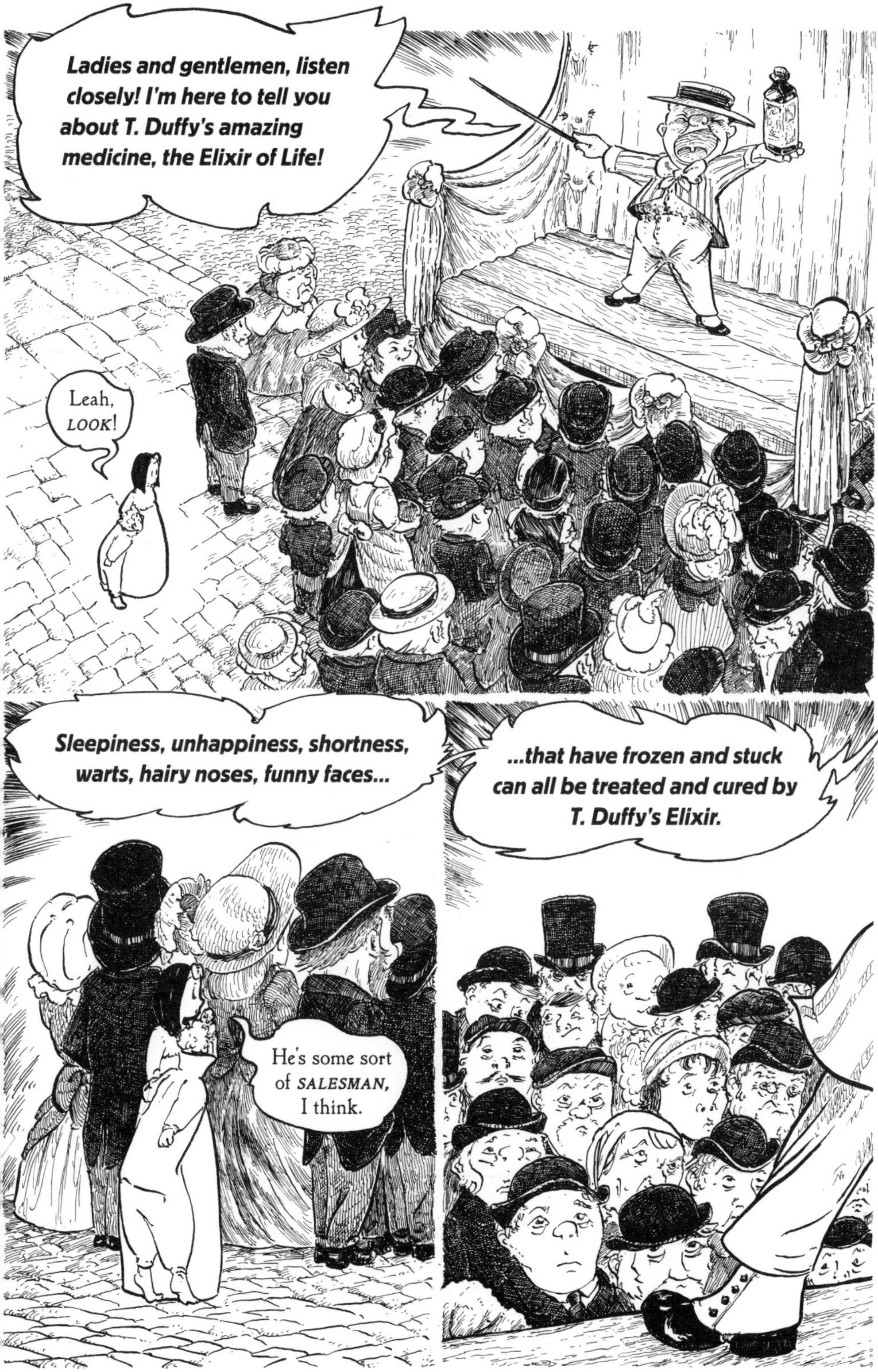
Ladies and gentlemen, listen closely! I'm here to tell you about T. Duffy's amazing medicine, the Elixir of Life!
Leah, LOOK!
Sleepiness, unhappiness, shortness, warts, hairy noses, funny faces...
He's some sort of SALESMAN, I think.
...that have frozen and stuck can all be treated and cured by T. Duffy's Elixir.

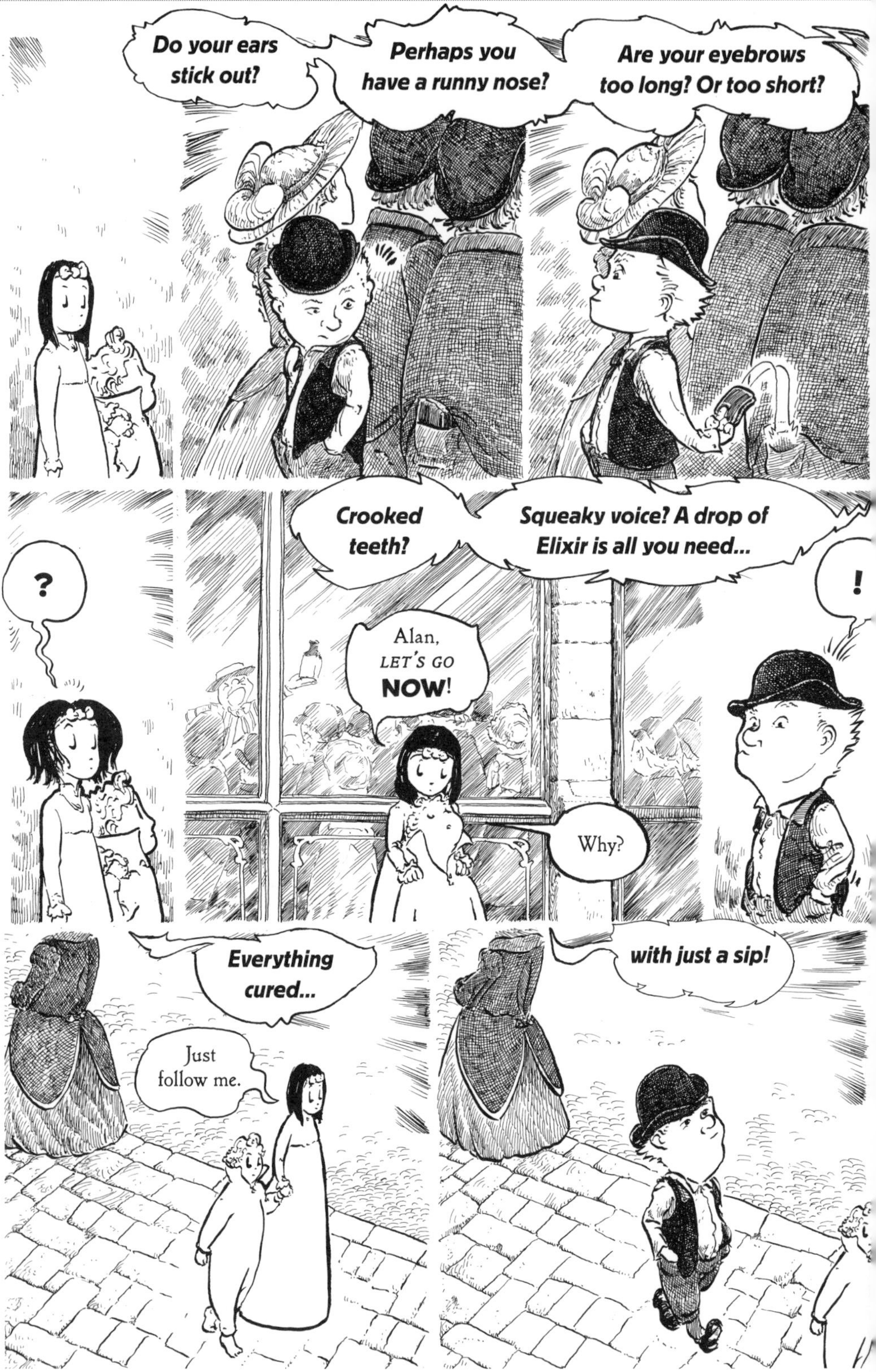
Do your ears stick out?
Perhaps you have a runny nose?
Are your eyebrows too long? Or too short?
?
Crooked teeth?
Squeaky voice? A drop of Elixir is all you need...
!
Alan, LET'S GO NOW!
Why?
Everything cured...
Just follow me.
with just a sip!

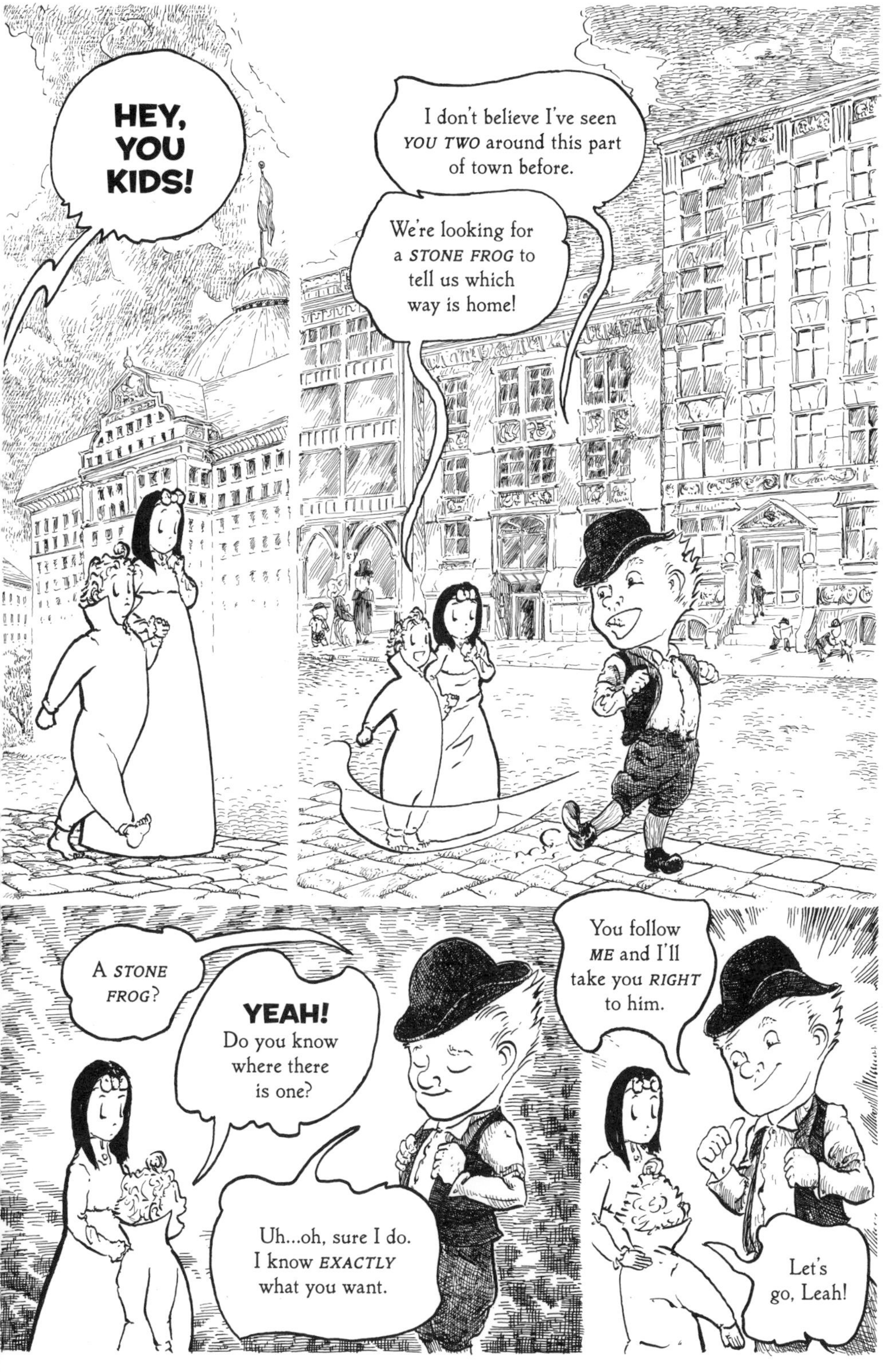

HEY, YOU KIDS!
I don't believe I've seen YOU TWO around this part of town before.
We're looking for a STONE FROG to tell us which way is home!
A STONE FROG?
YEAH! Do you know where there is one?
Uh...oh, sure I do. I know EXACTLY what you want.
You follow ME and I'll take you RIGHT to him.
Let's go, Leah!

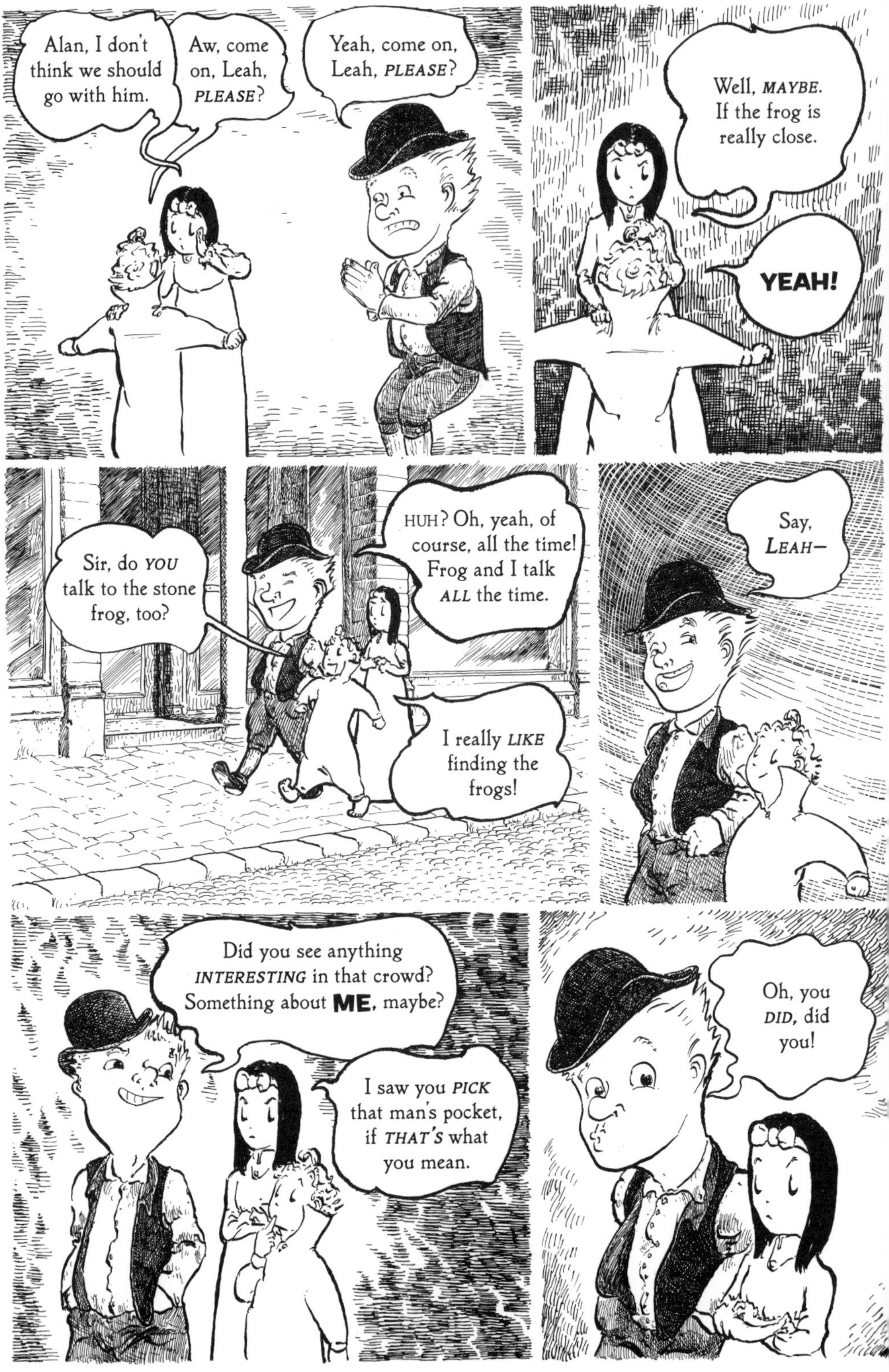

Alan, I don't think we should go with him.
Aw, come on, Leah, PLEASE?
Yeah, come on, Leah, PLEASE?
Well, MAYBE. If the frog is really close.
YEAH!
Sir, do YOU talk to the stone frog, too?
HUH? Oh, yeah, of course, all the time! Frog and I talk ALL the time.
I really LIKE finding the frogs!
Say, LEAH—
Did you see anything INTERESTING in that crowd? Something about ME, maybe?
I saw you PICK that man's pocket, if THAT'S what you mean.
Oh, you DID, did you!

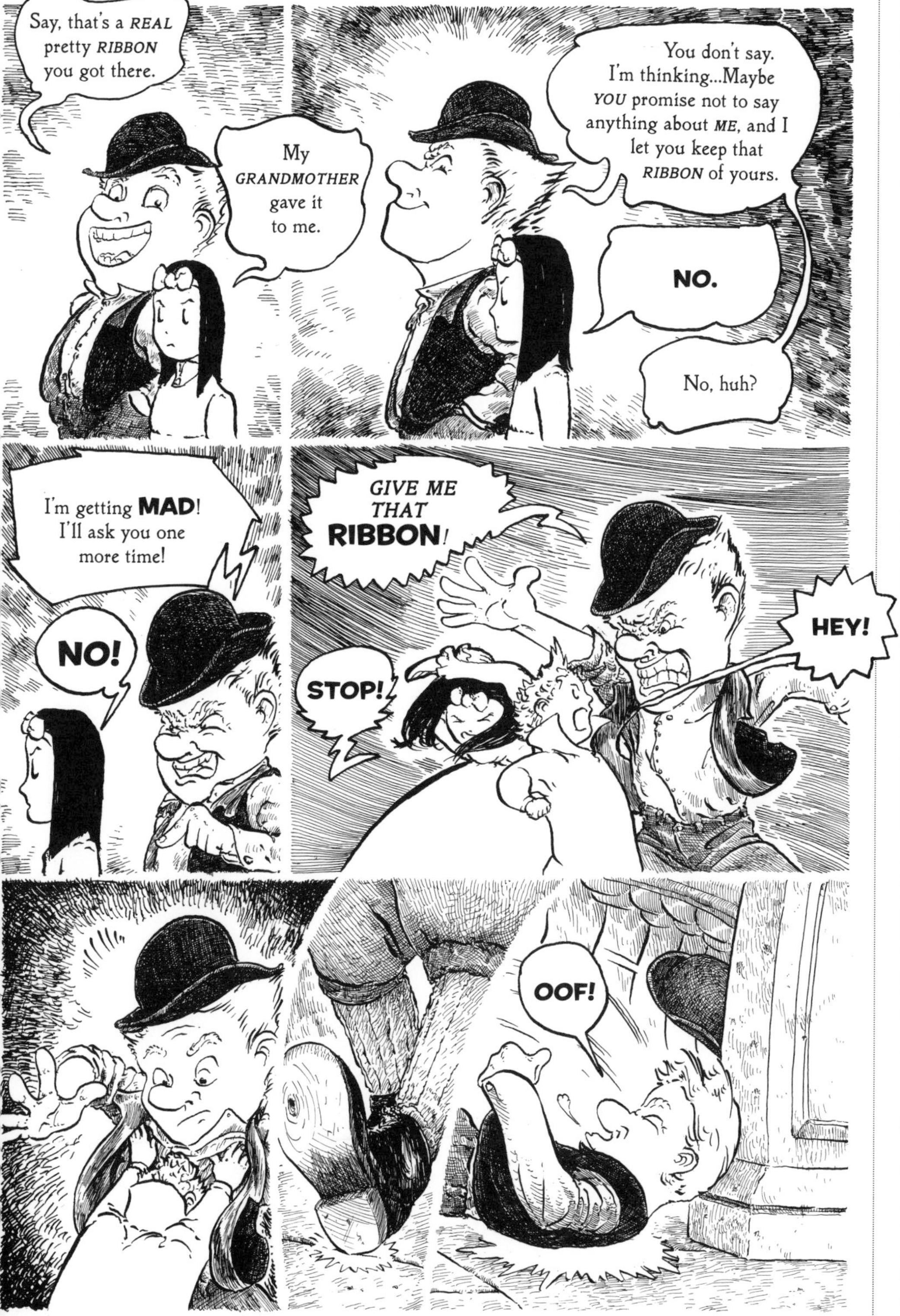

Say, that's a REAL pretty RIBBON you got there.
My GRANDMOTHER gave it to me.
You don't say. I'm thinking...Maybe YOU promise not to say anything about ME, and I let you keep that RIBBON of yours.
NO.
No, huh?
I'm getting MAD! I'll ask you one more time!
NO!
GIVE ME THAT RIBBON!
HEY!
STOP!
OOF!

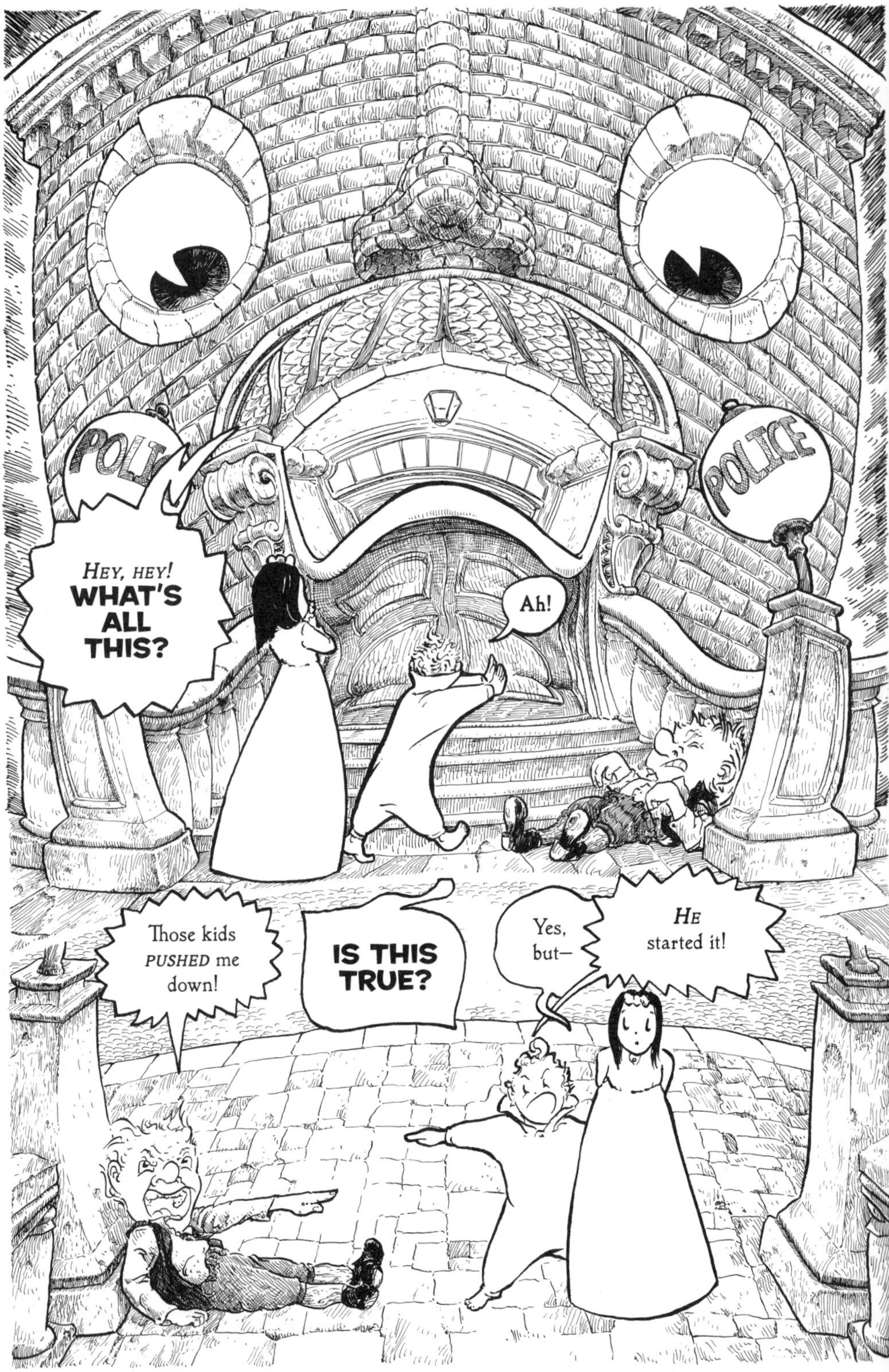
POLICE
POLICE
Hey, hey! **WHAT'S ALL THIS?**
Ah!
Those kids *PUSHED* me down!
IS THIS TRUE?
Yes, but—
He started it!

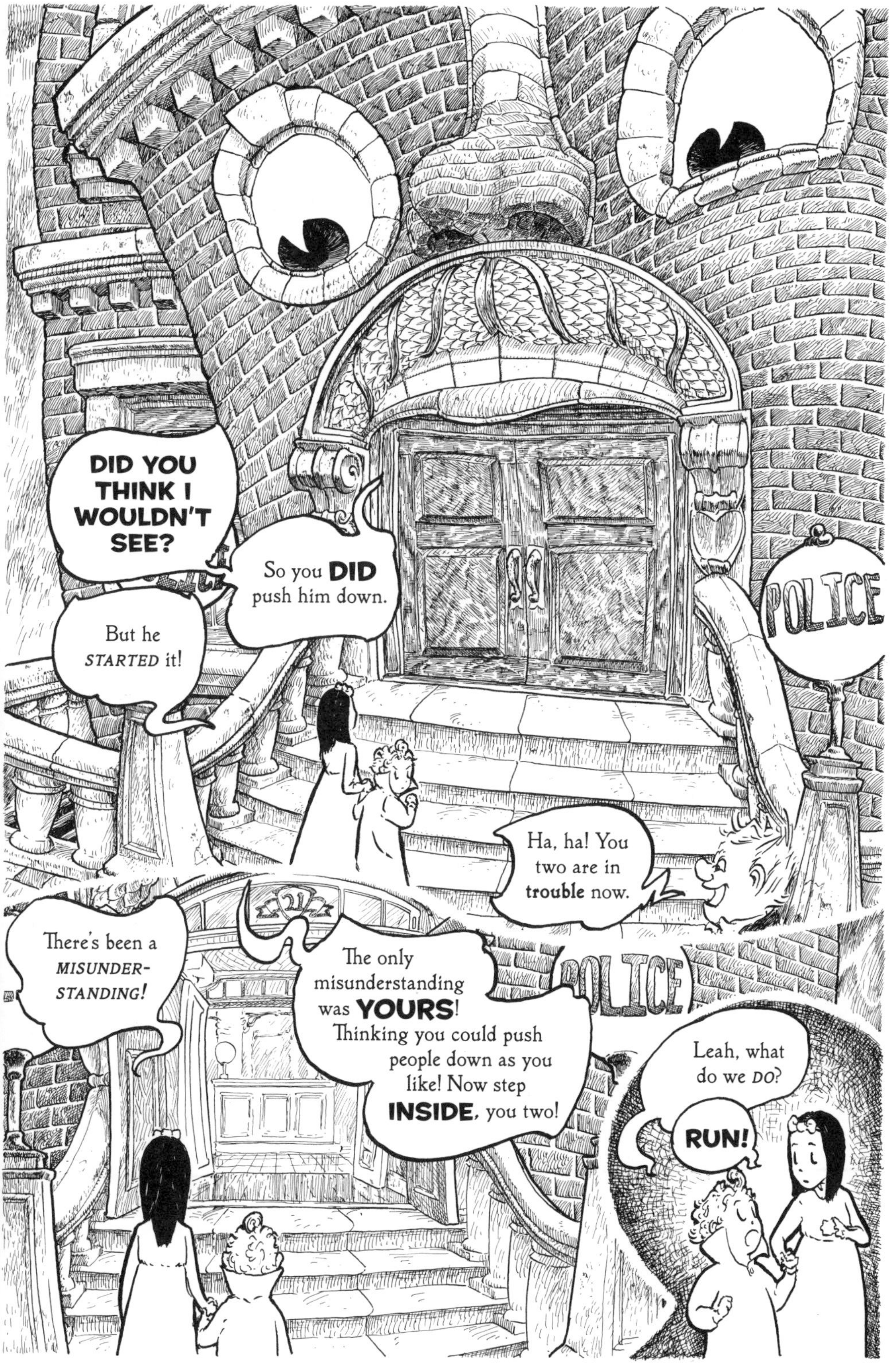

DID YOU THINK I WOULDN'T SEE?
So you DID push him down.
But he STARTED it!
POLICE
Ha, ha! You two are in trouble now.
There's been a MISUNDER-STANDING!
The only misunderstanding was YOURS! Thinking you could push people down as you like! Now step INSIDE, you two!
POLICE
Leah, what do we DO?
RUN!

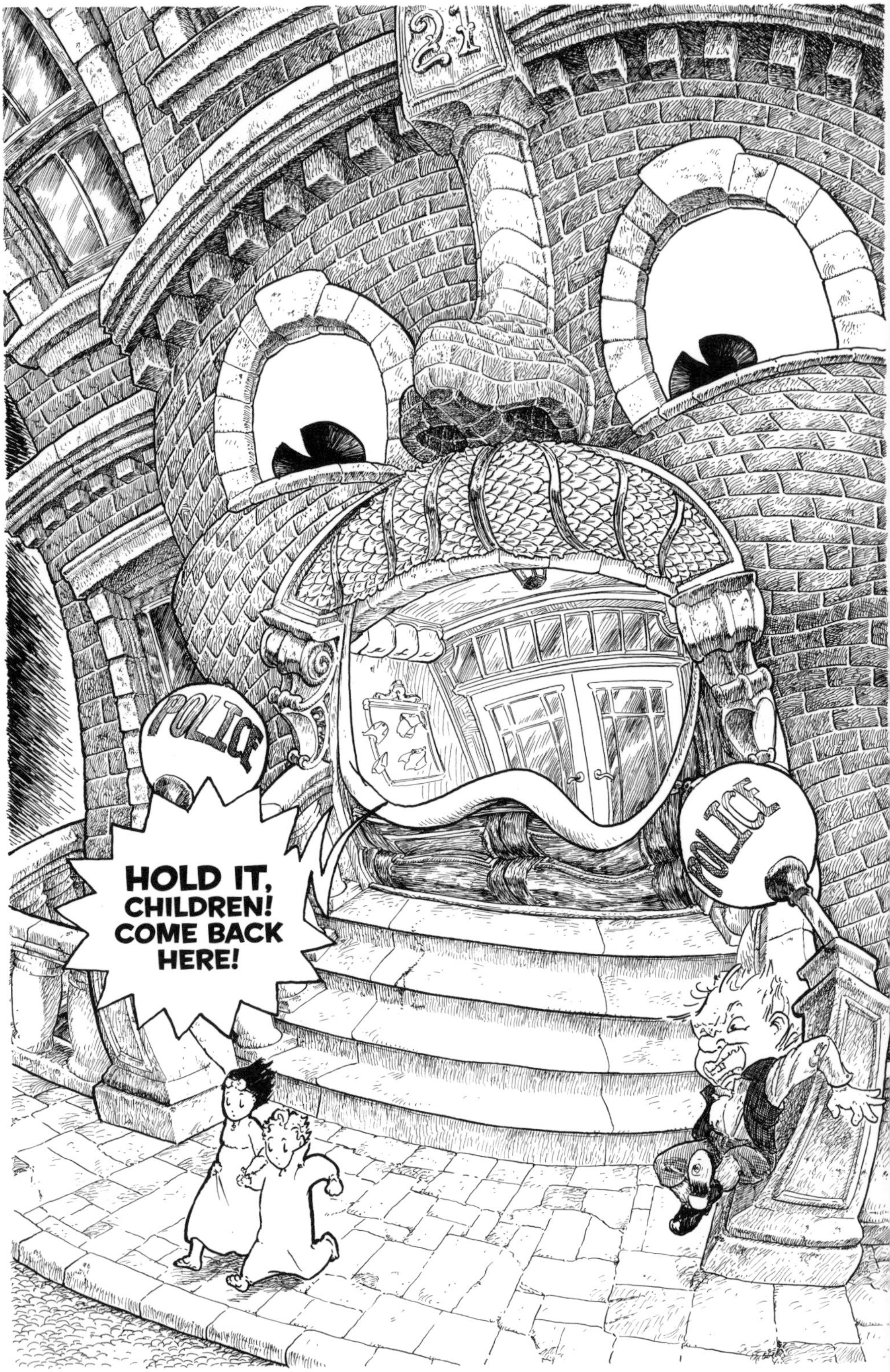
21
POLICE
POLICE
HOLD IT, CHILDREN! COME BACK HERE!

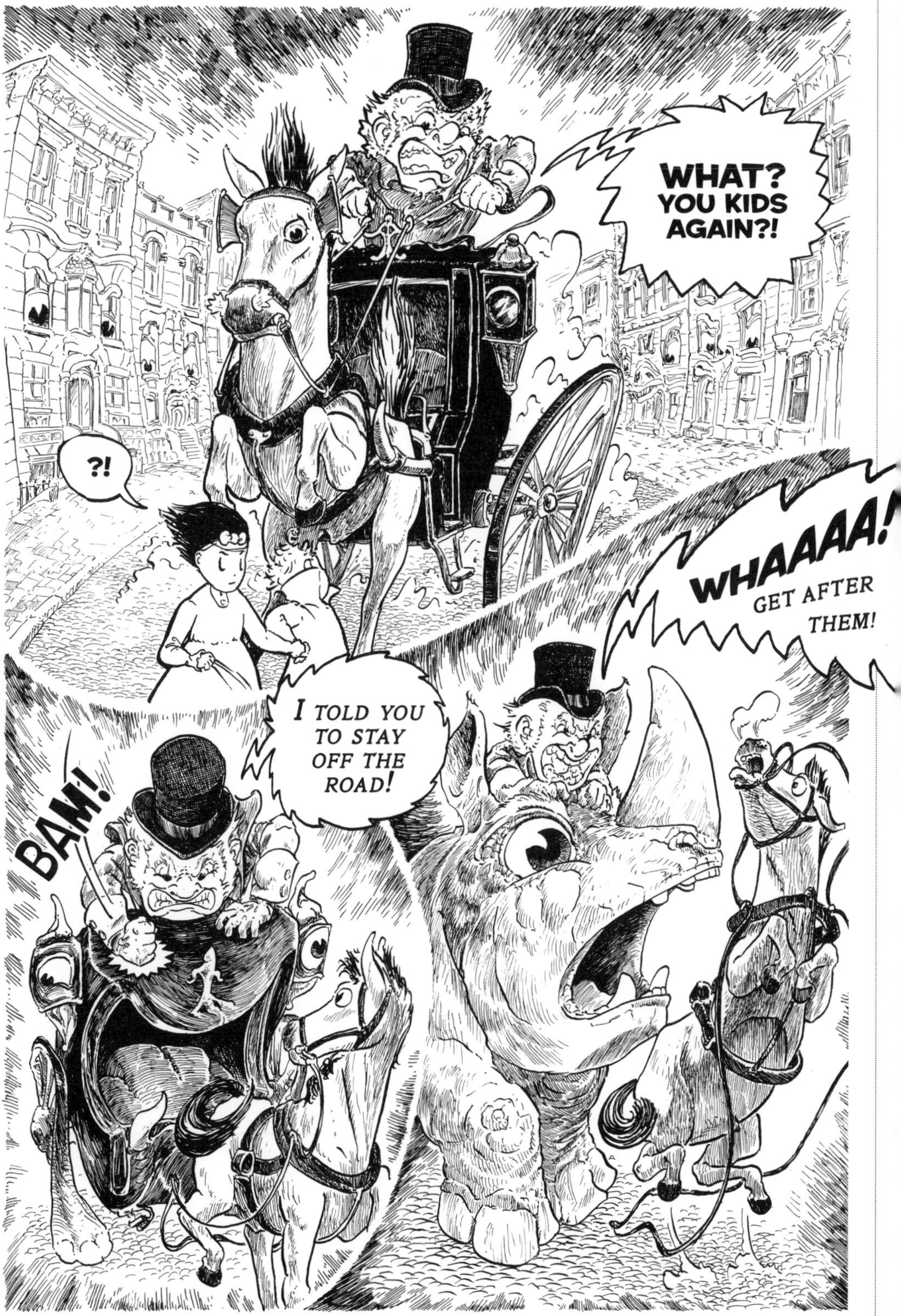
WHAT? YOU KIDS AGAIN?!
?!
WHAAAA!
GET AFTER THEM!
I TOLD YOU TO STAY OFF THE ROAD!
BAM!

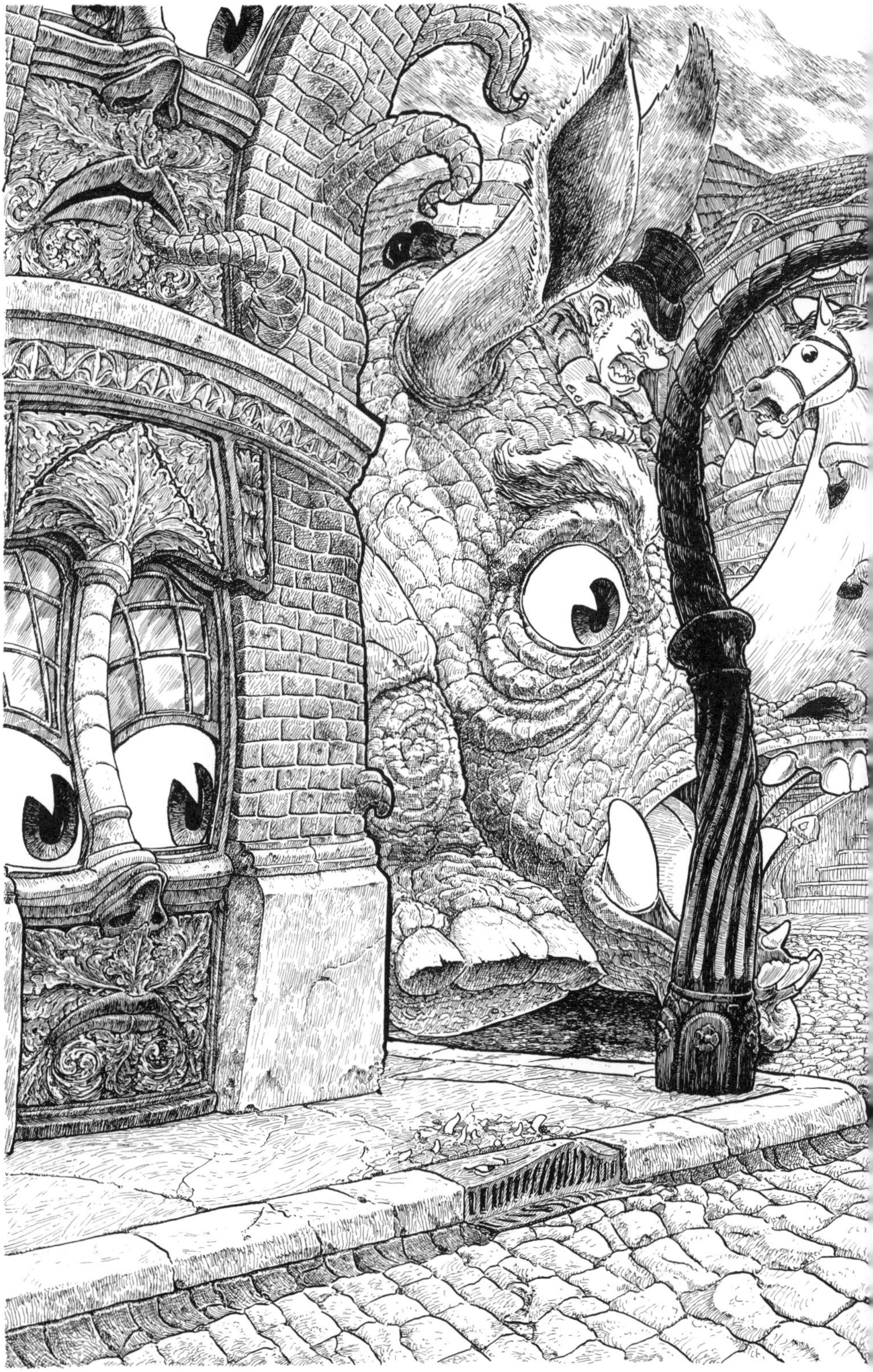

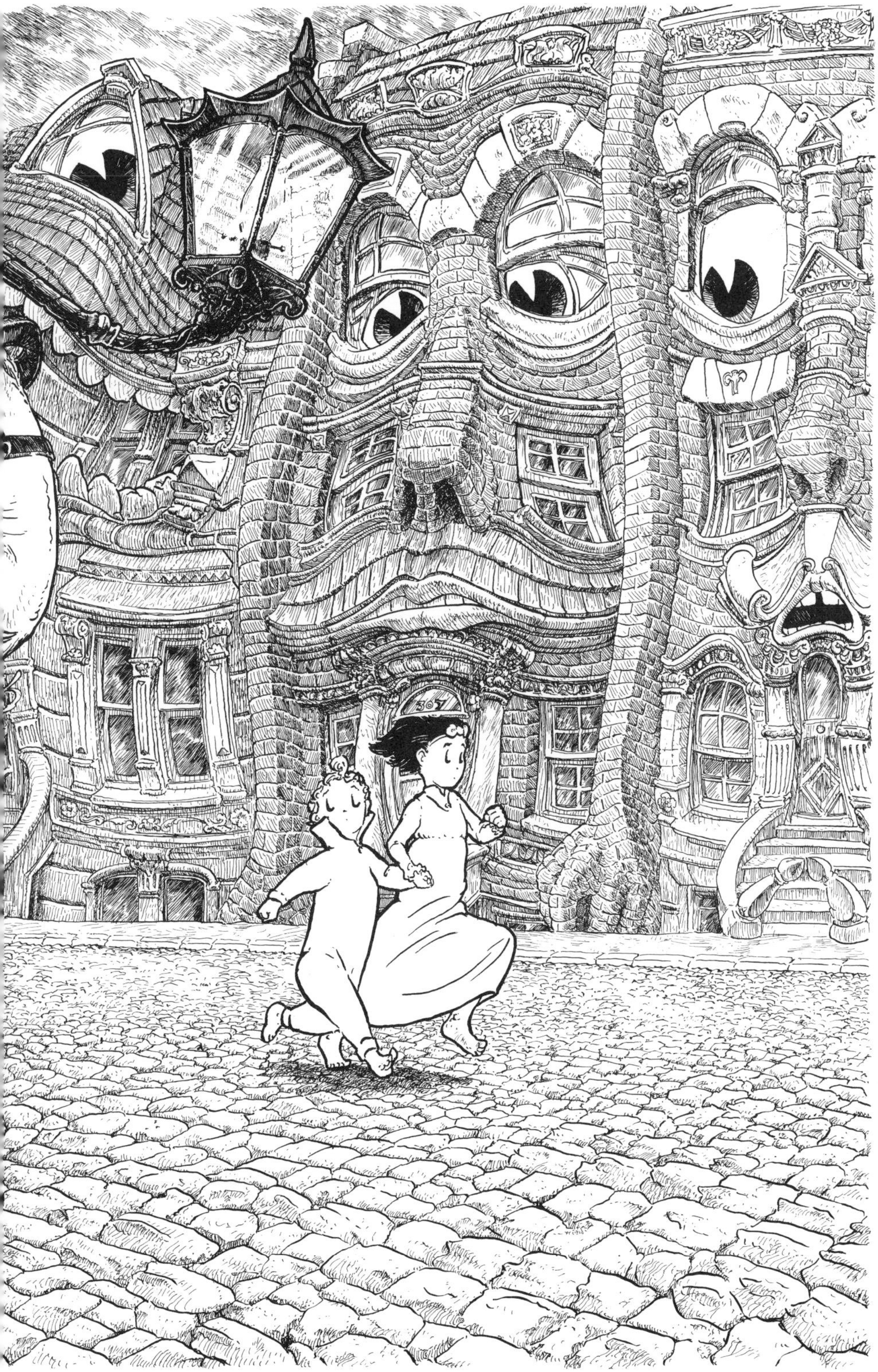

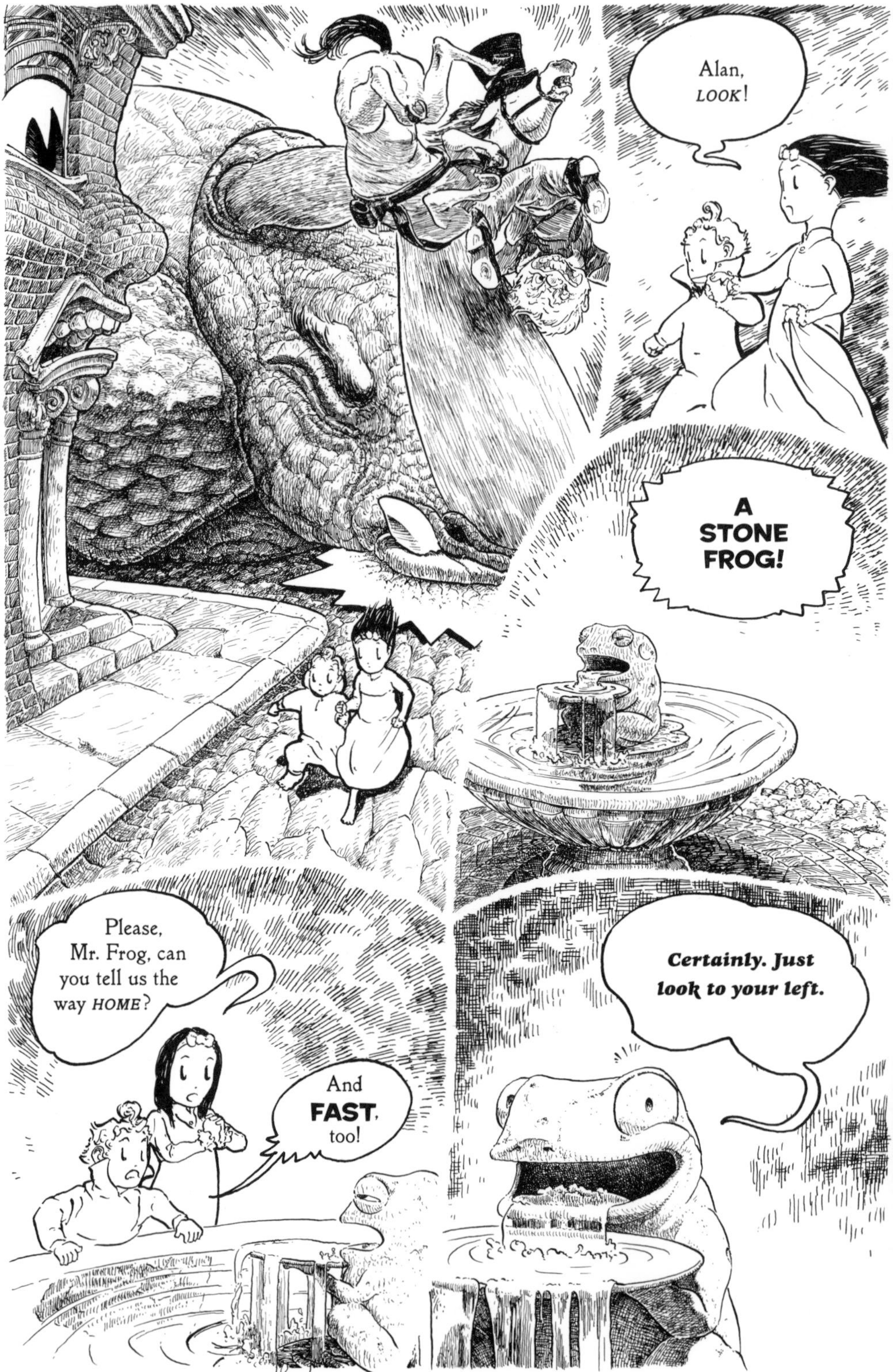
Alan, LOOK!
A STONE FROG!
Please, Mr. Frog, can you tell us the way HOME?
And FAST, too!
Certainly. Just look to your left.

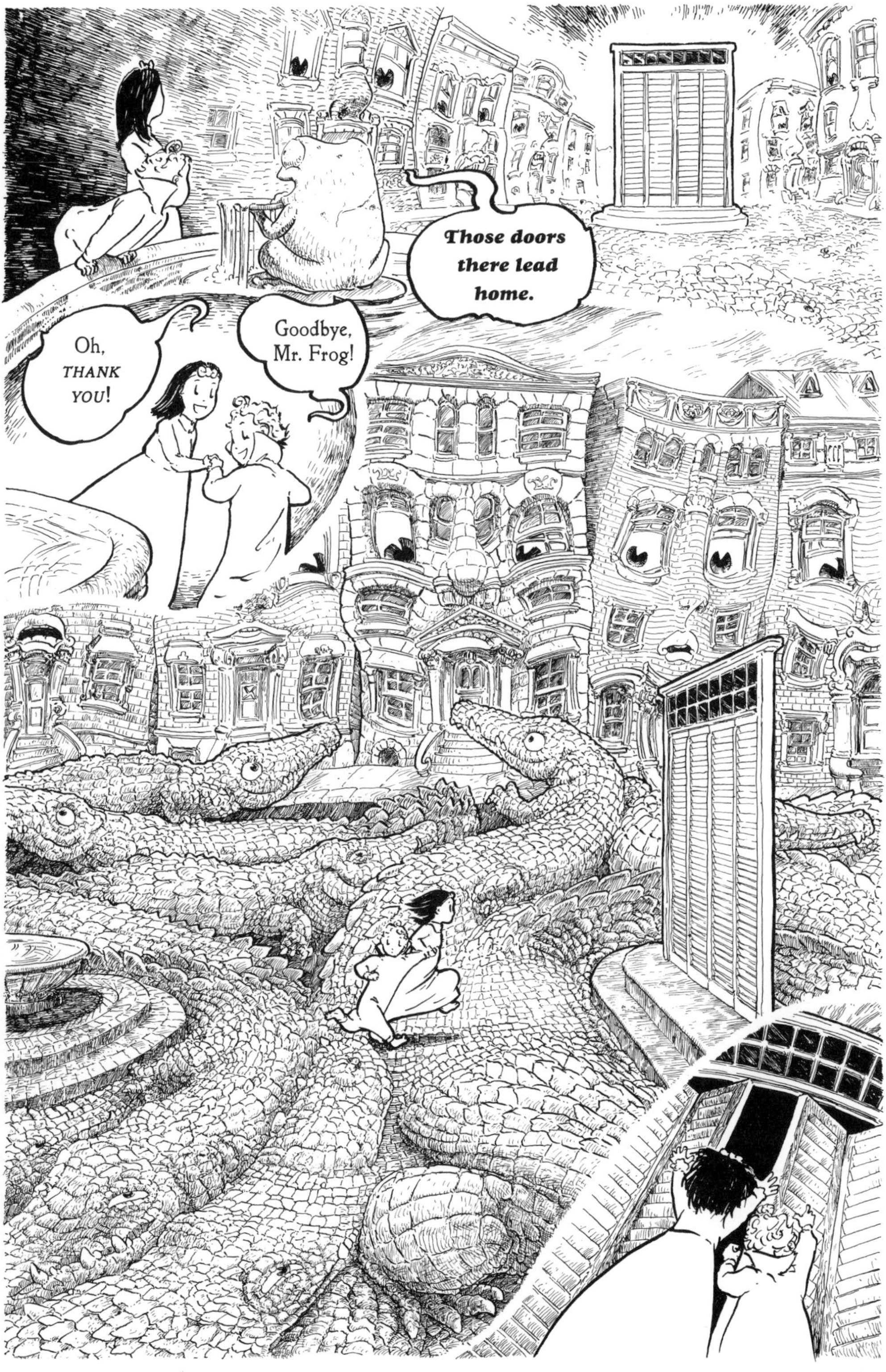
Those doors there lead home.
Oh, THANK YOU!
Goodbye, Mr. Frog!

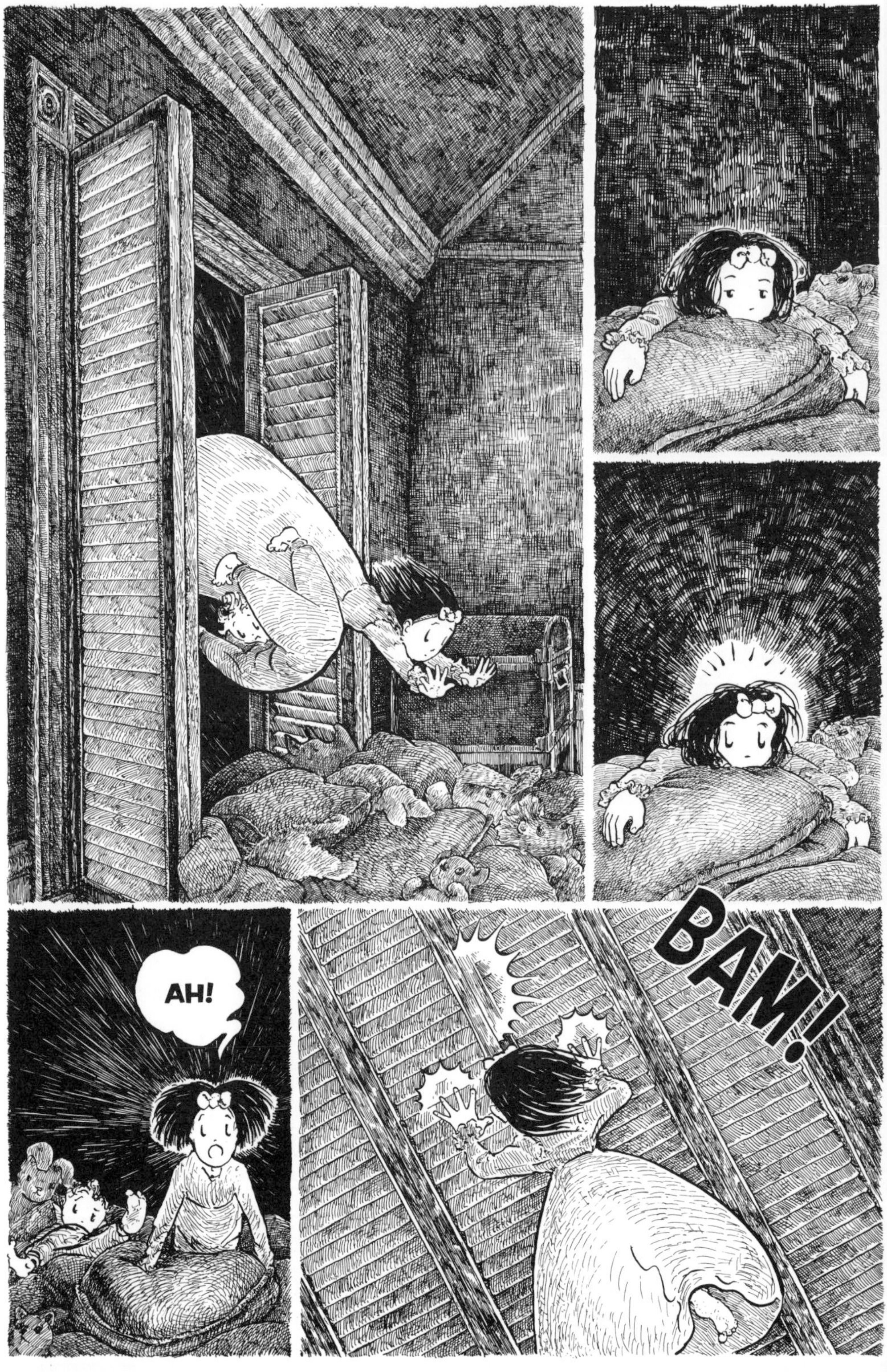
AH!
BAM!

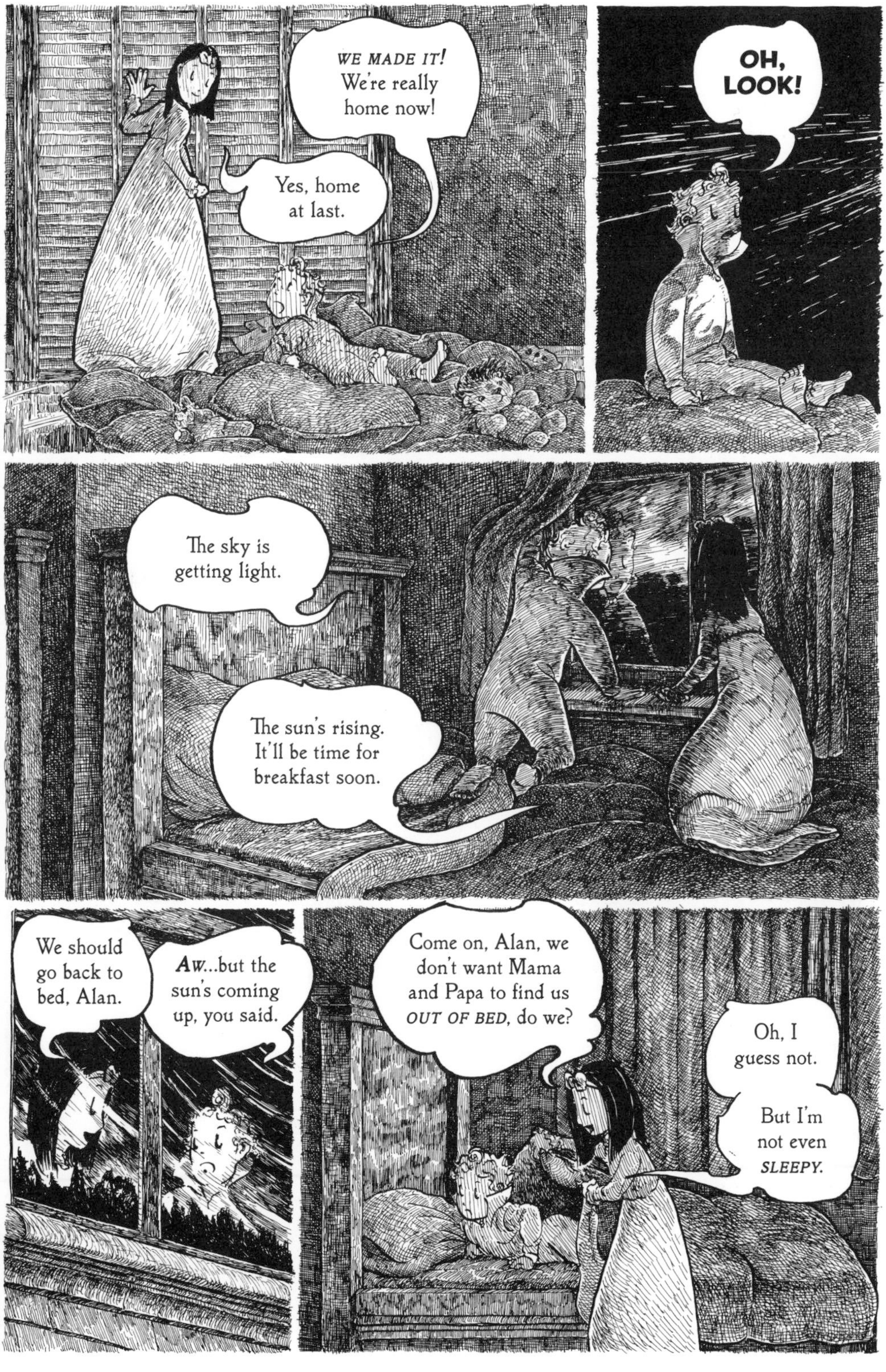
WE MADE IT! We're really home now!
Yes, home at last.
OH, LOOK!
The sky is getting light.
The sun's rising. It'll be time for breakfast soon.
We should go back to bed, Alan.
AW...but the sun's coming up, you said.
Come on, Alan, we don't want Mama and Papa to find us OUT OF BED, do we?
Oh, I guess not.
But I'm not even SLEEPY.

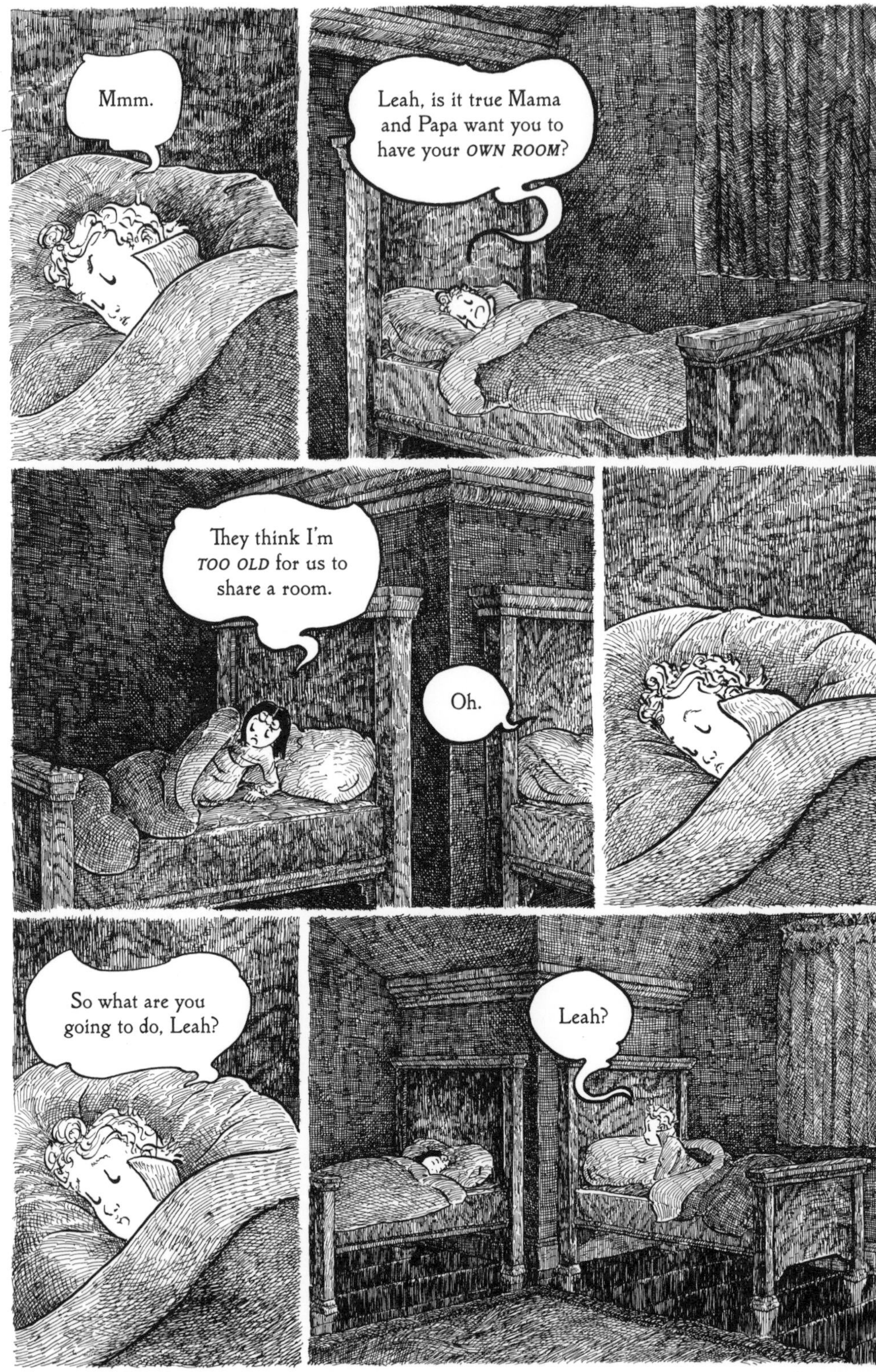
Mmm.
Leah, is it true Mama and Papa want you to have your OWN ROOM?
They think I'm TOO OLD for us to share a room.
Oh.
So what are you going to do, Leah?
Leah?

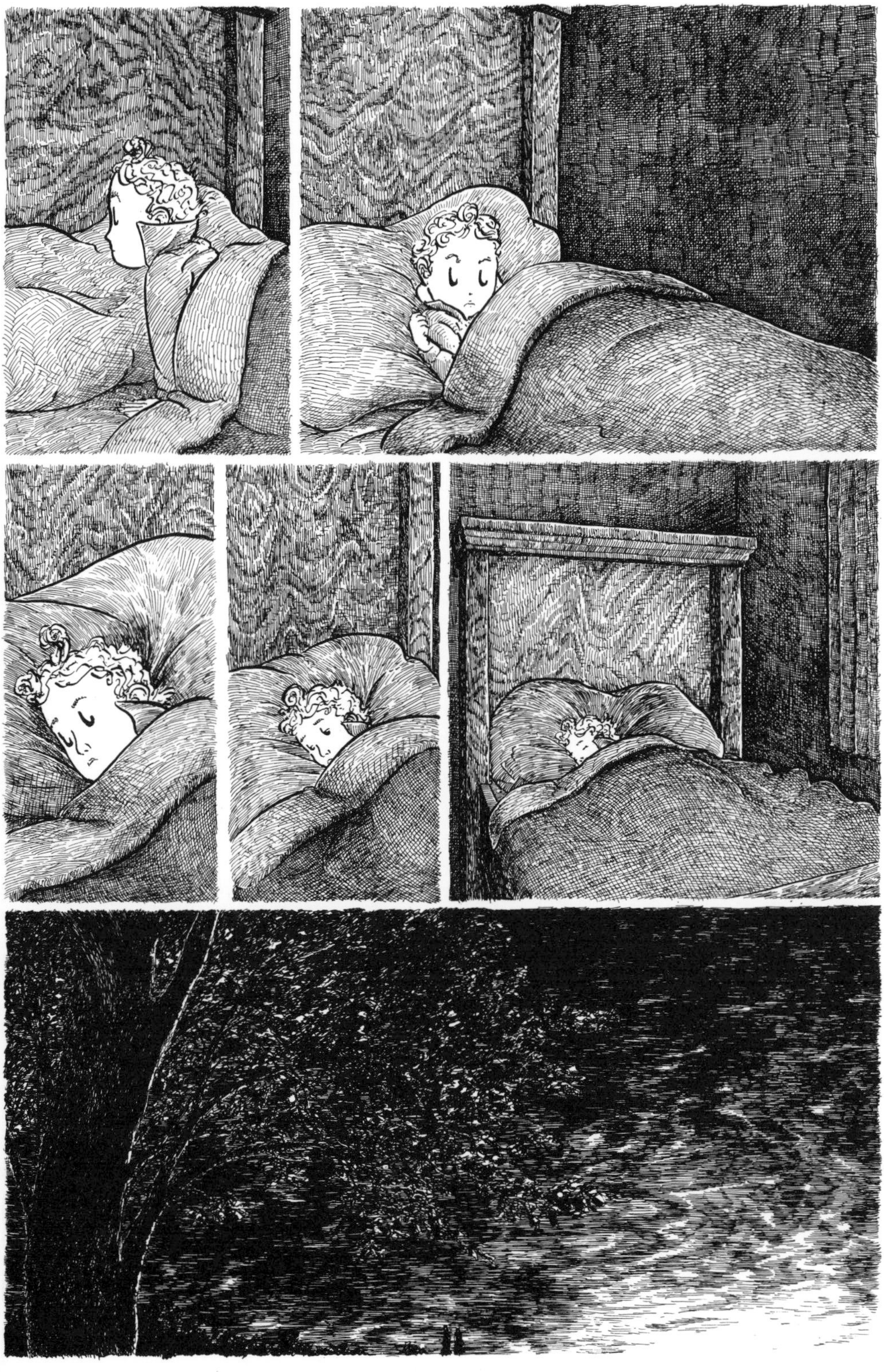

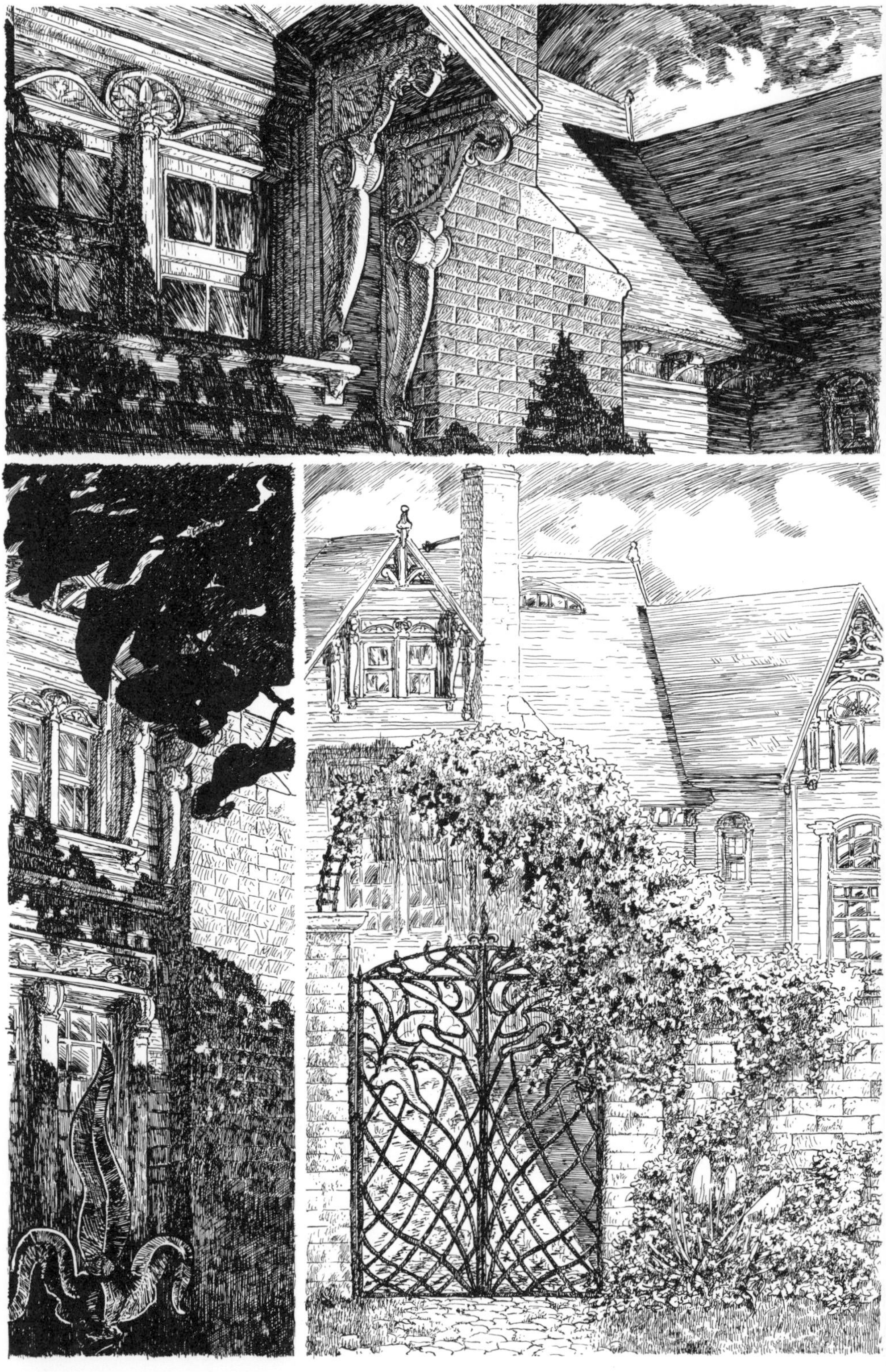

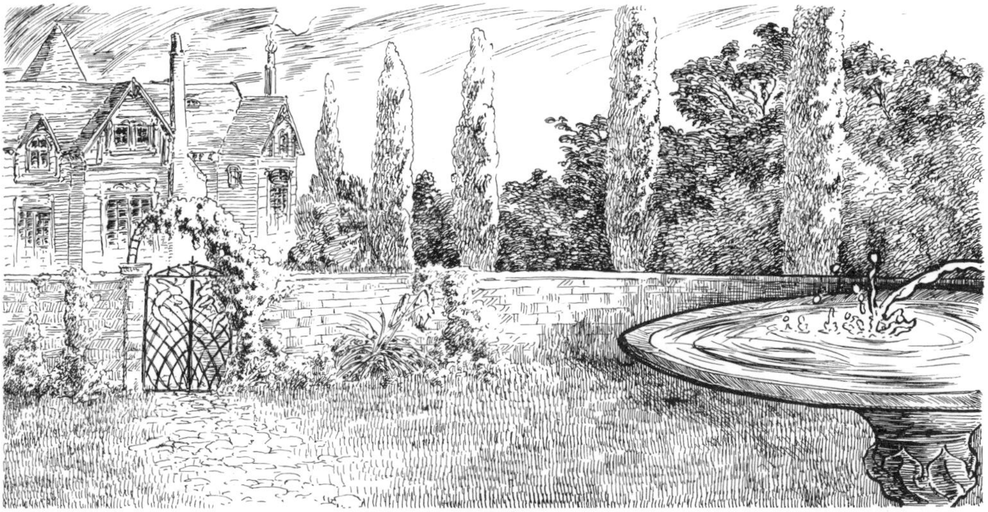

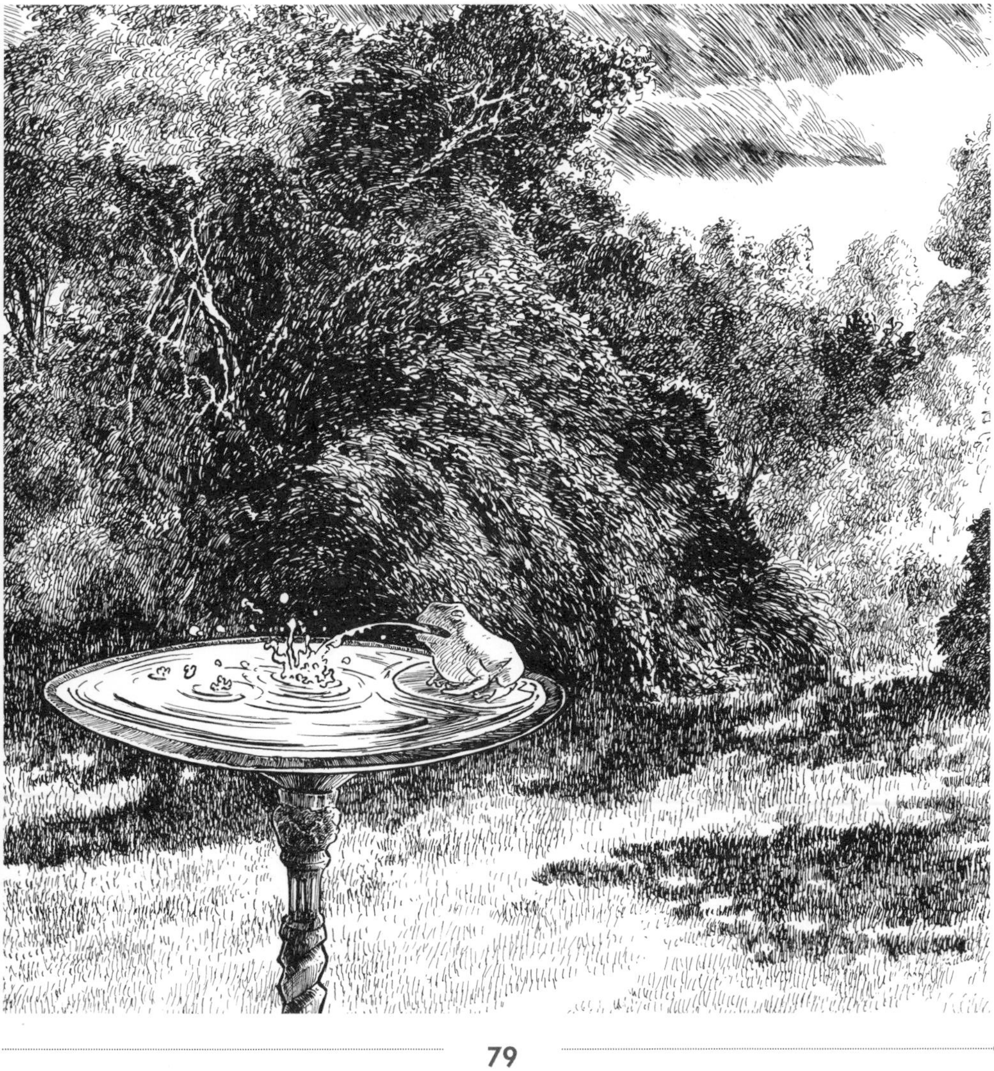

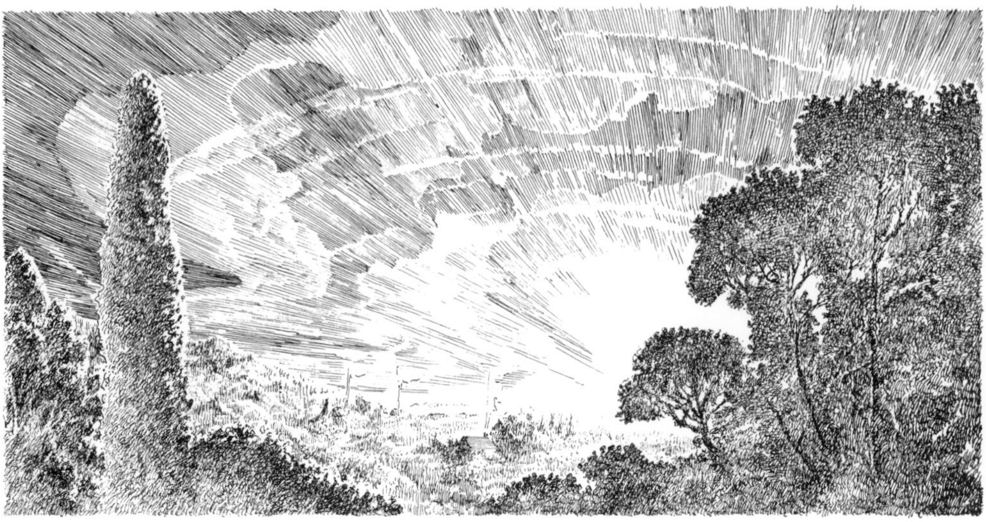

ABOUT THE AUTHOR

DAVID NYTRA has been drawing since he was old enough to hold a pencil. An artist who works in many media, including clay, wood, and animation, he lives in the small town of 100 Mile House in British Columbia, Canada. This is his first children's book. His second graphic novel for TOON, *Windmill Dragons*, was published in 2015. Though his own dreams are often unexciting and he's only a little bit allergic to bees, he loved books with many creatures in them as a child and he hopes he has put enough beasties in here to satisfy even the most demanding reader.

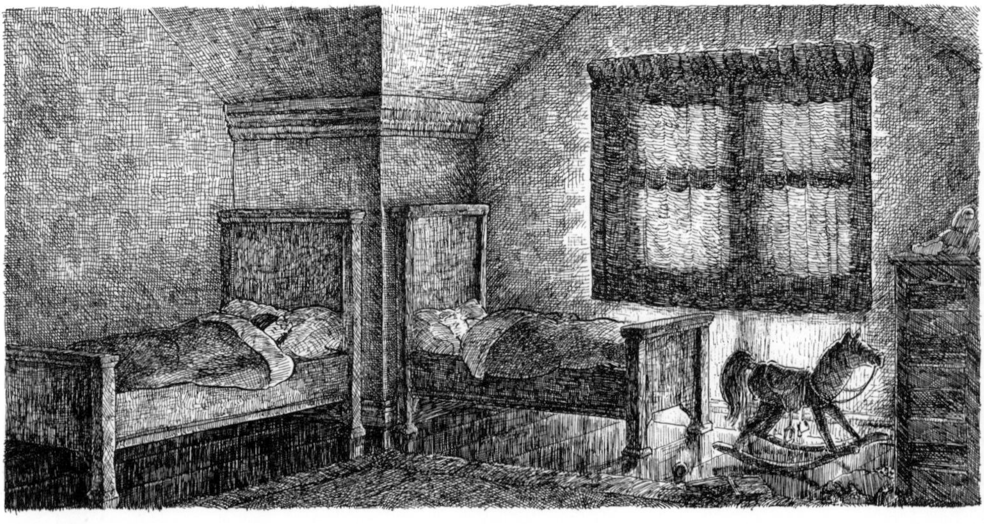